The Christmas Mystery

JOSTEIN GAARDER

The Christmas Mystery

Translated by Elizabeth Rokkan

Illustrated by Sarah Gibb

Orion
Children's Books

This abridged edition first published 2002
First published in Great Britain in 1996
and as a Dolphin paperback in 1998
by Orion Children's Books
a division of the Orion Publishing Group Ltd
Orion House
5 Upper St Martin's Lane
London WC2H 9EA

Originally published in Norwegian
under the title *Julemysteriet*,
copyright © 1992 by H. Aschehoug & Co
(W. Nygaard), Oslo

A catalogue record for this book is available from the British Library.
Printed and bound in Italy
ISBN 1 84255 050 0

Contents

The 1st *
of December

DUSK WAS FALLING. The lights were on in the Christmas streets, thick snowflakes were dancing between the lamps. The streets were crowded with people.

Among all these busy persons were Papa and Joachim, who had gone into town to buy an Advent calendar. It was their last chance, because tomorrow would be the first of December. They were sold out at the newsstand and in the big bookstore at the market.

Joachim tugged his father's hand hard and pointed at a tiny shop window where a brightly coloured Advent calendar was leaning against a pile of books.

'There!' he said.

Papa turned back. 'Saved!'

They went into a little bookshop that Joachim thought looked old and worn out. Books stood tightly packed on shelves along all the walls from floor to ceiling, all of them different.

A large pile of Advent calendars lay on the counter. There were two kinds, one with a picture of Santa Claus with a sledge and reindeer and the other with a picture of a barn with a tiny little elf eating porridge out of a big bowl.

Papa held up the two calendars.

'There are plastic figures in this one and chocolate ones in that,' he said.

Joachim examined the two calendars. He didn't know which one he wanted.

'It was different when I was a boy,' continued Papa. 'Then there was only a tiny picture behind each door, one for each day. But it was exciting every morning, trying to guess what the picture would be. When we opened it … well … it was like opening the door to a different world.'

Joachim had noticed something. He pointed to one of the walls of books. 'There's an Advent calendar over there too.'

He ran over to fetch it and held it up to show Papa. It had a picture of Joseph and Mary bending over the baby Jesus in the manger. The three Wise Men from the East were kneeling in the background. Outside the stable were the shepherds with their sheep, and angels floating down from the sky. One of them was blowing a trumpet.

The colours of the calendar were faded as if it had been lying in the sun all summer, but the picture was so beautiful that Joachim almost felt sorry for it.

'I want this one,' he said.

Papa smiled. 'You know, I don't think this one's for sale.

I think it must be very old. Maybe as old as I am.'

Joachim wouldn't give up. 'None of the doors are open.'

'But it's only here on display.'

'I want it,' repeated Joachim.

The bookseller came up – a man with white hair. He looked surprised when he saw the Advent calendar.

'Beautiful!' he exclaimed. 'And genuine – yes, original. It almost looks home-made.'

'He wants to buy it,' explained Papa, pointing at Joachim. 'I'm trying to explain that it's not for sale.'

The man raised his eyebrows.

'Did you find it here? I haven't seen one like that for years.'

'It was in front of all the books,' said Joachim.

'Oh, it must be old John up to his tricks again,' said the bookseller.

Papa stared at the man. 'John?'

'Yes, he's a strange character. He sells roses in the market, but where he gets them from, nobody knows. Sometimes he comes in and asks for a glass of water. In summer when it's hot he'll pour the last drops over his head before he goes out again. He's poured a few drops over me a couple of times, too. To thank me for the water he sometimes leaves one

9

or two roses on the counter; or he'll put an old book on the bookshelf. Once he put a photograph of a young woman in the window. It was from a country far away – maybe that's where he comes from himself. "Elisabet", it said on the photo.'

'And now he's left an Advent calendar?'

'Yes, evidently.'

'There's something written on it,' said Joachim. He read aloud, 'MAGIC ADVENT CALENDAR. Price 75 øre.'

The bookseller nodded. 'In that case it must be very old.'

'May I buy it for 75 øre?' asked Joachim.

The man laughed. 'I think you should have it for nothing. You'll see, old John had you in mind.'

'Thank you, thank you, thank you,' replied Joachim, on his way out of the bookshop already.

Papa shook the bookseller's hand and followed Joachim out on to the pavement.

Joachim hugged the calendar tight. 'I'll open it tomorrow,' he said.

Joachim kept waking up that night, thinking about the bookseller and John with his roses. Most of all he thought about the magic Advent calendar. It was as old as Papa, but all the same, nobody had opened any of the doors. Before he went to bed he had found all the doors from 1 to 24. The twenty-fourth was of course Christmas Eve, and that door was four times bigger than the others, covering almost the whole of the manger in the stable.

Where had the magic Advent calendar been for over forty

years? And what would happen when he opened the first door?

When he woke up again and it was seven o'clock, he reached up for the calendar, which was hanging above his bed, to open the first door. His fingers were so impatient and nervous that it was difficult to get hold of it properly. At last he managed to loosen a tiny corner, and the door opened slowly.

Joachim gazed in to a picture of a toyshop. Among all the toys and the people were a little lamb and a small girl, but he couldn't look at the picture in detail, for just as he opened the door something fell out on to his bed. He bent down and picked it up.

It was a thin sheet of paper, folded over and over. When he had smoothed it out he saw that there was writing on both sides. So he read what was on the paper.

 THE LAMBKIN

'Elisabet!' her mother called after her. 'Come back, Elisabet!'

Elisabet Hansen had been standing staring at the big pile of teddy bears and furry animals while her mother was buying Christmas presents. All of a sudden a little lamb shot out of the pile. It jumped on to the floor and looked around. It had a bell round its neck, and the bell started to jingle.

How could a toy suddenly come to life? Elisabet was so surprised that she started to chase the lamb. It was running across the wide floor of the department store in the direction of the moving staircase.

'Lambkin, lambkin!' she called after it.

'Come back, Elisabet!' repeated her mother severely.

But Elisabet had already jumped on to the moving staircase. She could see the lamb running through the ground floor where they sold underwear and ties.

As soon as she had solid ground beneath her feet again, she went the same way as the lamb. It had managed to bound out on to the street where the snowflakes were dancing among the chains of Christmas lights. Elisabet knocked over a stand of winter gloves and followed it.

Out in the noisy street she could barely hear the bell jingling. But Elisabet did not give up. She was determined to stroke the lamb's soft fleece.

'Lambkin, lambkin!'

The lamb sprang across the road against a red light. The cars tooted their horns, and a motorbike had to swerve on to the pavement. The lamb didn't stop, so Elisabet couldn't stop either.

As they ran, Elisabet heard the church clock striking three. She noticed it specially, because she knew she had come to town on the five o'clock bus. Perhaps the hands had become so tired of going in the same direction year after year that they had suddenly begun to go the opposite way instead.

But there was something else as well. When Elisabet had

gone into the department store, it had been almost completely dark. Now it was suddenly light again, and that was curious, because there had been no night in between.

As soon as the lamb had a chance, it found a road leading out of town, and trotted on towards a small wood. It sprang on to a path between tall pine trees. Now the lamb had to slow down a little, for the path was covered with all the snow that had been falling during the past few days.

Elisabet went after it. It was difficult for her to run now, too. Her mother's cries had been drowned long ago by the noise in the street and soon she couldn't even hear street sounds.

Joachim looked up from the sheet of paper that had fallen out of the magic Advent calendar. What he had read was so amazing.

He had always liked secrets. Now he remembered the little box with the key in it, the one Grandma had bought him in Poland. He put the paper from the Advent calendar there, turned the key, and hid it under his pillow.

So when Mama and Papa woke up and came to look at the Advent calendar too, they only saw the picture of the lamb in the department store.

'Do you remember?' asked Mama, looking up at Papa. 'It was just like that when we were small.'

Papa nodded. 'Then we could use our imagination on the little picture and make up the rest ourselves.'

Something was laughing inside Joachim. Only he knew that there had been a mysterious piece of paper inside the calendar.

For the rest of the day Joachim wondered whether Elisabet would catch up with the lamb so that she could stroke its fleece. Would he find out tomorrow?

For then there'd surely be another little piece of paper?

⋆ The 2nd ⋆
of December

JOACHIM WOKE UP before Mama and Papa the next morning too. He sat up and looked at the Advent calendar. Only now did he notice a little lamb lying at the feet of one of the shepherds. Wasn't that strange? He had spent a long time looking at the picture with all the angels and the Wise Men, the shepherds and their sheep, but he had never noticed the lamb.

Perhaps it was because he had read about the lamb on the piece of paper that had fallen out of the calendar. But *that* lamb had jumped out of a modern shop – and the lamb on the Advent calendar had lived in Bethlehem, long ago.

Now he found the door with a number 2 on it, and opened it carefully. A folded piece of paper fell out of the calendar as the door slowly opened. He peeped in at a picture of a wood, where an angel stood with his arm round a little girl.

Joachim bent down and picked up the scrap of paper that had fallen into the bed. He unfolded it and began to read.

 EPHIRIEL

Elisabet Hansen didn't know how far nor how long she had run after the lamb, but when she set off through the town it had been snowing heavily. Now it had not only stopped snowing, there was no snow on the path either. Among the trees she could see blue anemones, coltsfoot and windflowers, and that was unusual, because it was very nearly Christmas.

It occurred to Elisabet that perhaps she had run so far that she had reached a country where it was summer all the year round. If not, she must have run for so long that spring and the warm weather had arrived already. In that case what would have happened to Christmas?

While she stood wondering she heard the tinkle of a bell in the distance. Elisabet started running again and soon caught sight of the lamb. It had found a small grassy bank and was grazing on it greedily.

Elisabet crept up towards the lamb, but just as she was about to pounce on it in order to stroke it, it sprang away again.

'Lambkin, lambkin!'

Elisabet tried to keep up with it, but she tripped over a pine root and fell flat on the ground.

When she looked up she caught sight of a shining figure between the trees. Elisabet looked, wide-eyed, for it was neither an animal nor a human being. A pair of wings were sticking out of a robe as white as the lamb.

Elisabet realised at once that the shining figure must be an angel. She had seen angels in books and pictures, but it was the first time she had seen one in real life.

'Fear not!' said the angel in a gentle voice.

Elisabet raised herself halfway up.

'You needn't think I'm afraid of you,' she replied, a little sulkily because she had fallen and hurt herself.

The angel knelt down and stroked her gently on the nape of her neck with the tip of one of his wings.

'I said, "Fear not", to be on the safe side,' he said. 'We don't appear to humans very often, so it's best to be careful when we do. Usually people are frightened when they're visited by an angel.'

Suddenly Elisabet began to cry, not because she was afraid of angels, and not because she had hurt herself either. She didn't understand why she was crying until she heard herself sob, 'I wanted … to stroke the lamb.'

The angel nodded gracefully. 'I'm sure God wouldn't have created the lamb with such soft fleece unless He hoped someone would want to stroke it.'

'The lamb runs much faster than I do,' sobbed Elisabet, again, 'and it has twice as many legs too. Isn't that unfair? I can't see why a little lambkin should be in such a hurry.'

The angel helped her to her feet and said confidentially,

'It's going to Bethlehem.'

Elisabet had stopped crying. 'To Bethlehem?'

'Yes. To Bethlehem, to Bethlehem! For that's where Jesus was born.' Elisabet was very surprised at what the angel said.

'Then I want to go to Bethlehem,' she said.

The angel was dancing on the tips of his toes on the path.

'That suits me,' he said, hovering above the ground. 'I'm going there too. So we might just as well keep each other company, all three of us.'

Elisabet had learned that she should never go anywhere with people she didn't know. That certainly applied to angels as well. So she looked up at the angel and asked, 'What's your name?'

The angel curtseyed like a ballet dancer and said, 'My name is Ephiriel.'

Elisabet sniffed for the last time. Then she said, 'I don't think we have time to talk any more if we're going all the way to Bethlehem. Isn't it a long way?'

'Yes indeed, it's very far – and a very long time ago. But I know of a short cut, and that's the path we're taking now.'

And with that they began to run. First the lamb, then Elisabet. The angel Ephiriel danced behind them.

Joachim hid the piece of paper in the secret box for which
only he had the key.

It was John the flower-seller who had left the old calendar
with the bookseller. Did he know about the scraps of paper too?
Or was Joachim the only person in the whole world who knew
the secret?

But another thought struck him. Elisabet! he thought. Wasn't
Elisabet the name of the lady whose picture John had put in
the shop window?

Yes, it was, he was quite certain. Could it be the same
Elisabet he was reading about in the magic Advent calendar?
She was only a child, it's true, but the calendar was so old that
she must have had plenty of time to grow up during all the
years that had passed since then.

∗ The 3rd ∗
of December ∗

JOACHIM WOKE UP EARLY on the morning of the third of December. He pulled himself up in bed and peered up at the magic Advent calendar. At the top of the picture several angels were floating down through the clouds in the sky. One of them was blowing a trumpet.

Joachim imagined that the angel on the right of the picture must be Ephiriel. He was just as Joachim had thought Ephiriel might look, and he was smiling at Joachim, raising an arm as if he was trying to wave to him.

Joachim got to his feet on the bed and opened the door with the number 3 on it. He saw a tiny little picture of a vintage car. He had seen that kind of old car once when he went to the Technical Museum with Grandpa.

Joachim didn't understand what a vintage car could have to do with Christmas, but then he picked up the little piece of paper that had fallen out of the calendar. He snuggled down under the duvet and read what was written on the sheet.

 THE SECOND SHEEP

Elisabet and the angel Ephiriel ran on after the lamb. Soon they had left the wood behind and were going down a narrow country lane. In the distance thick smoke was rising from some tall factory chimneys.

'There's a town,' said Elisabet.

'That's Halden,' explained the angel. 'We're quite close to Sweden.' Suddenly they heard a clatter right behind them. Elisabet turned and saw an old car driving towards them. Driving the car was a man with a hat and coat and a black beard who looked a bit like the picture of Great-grandpa on the mantelpiece at home. As he passed, the man sounded the horn and doffed his hat.

'That car must be terribly old!' exclaimed Elisabet.

'On the contrary, I think it was probably brand new,' said Ephiriel.

'I always thought angels were much cleverer than humans. But you don't seem to know much about cars,' said Elisabet, sighing in frustration.

Ephiriel tried to hide a laugh. He pointed to a pile of logs.

'Sit down here,' he said. 'You deserve a short rest, and there's something important I have to tell you about our journey to Bethlehem.'

Elisabet sat down and looked at the angel.

'Now can you tell me exactly where we are going, my dear?' asked the angel.

'To Bethlehem,' replied Elisabet.

'And what are we going to do there?'

'We're going to stroke the lamb, I suppose.'

The angel nodded. 'And we'll also welcome the baby Jesus into the world. He was called God's lamb, because He was just as kind and innocent as the little lamb's fleece is soft. We have to travel two thousand years backwards in time to the moment when Jesus was born.'

Elisabet put her hand to her mouth. 'But isn't it impossible to travel backwards in time?' she asked.

'Not at all,' said Ephiriel. 'Nothing is impossible for God, and I am here as God's messenger. We have a small part of the journey behind us already. Down there you see Halden, and we have arrived back at the beginning of the twentieth century. Do you understand?'

'I think so,' said Elisabet. 'And that means the car wasn't old after all.'

'No. It may have been brand new. I'm sure you noticed how proud the driver was when he sounded his horn. Not very many people owned cars then.'

Elisabet simply sat and stared, and Ephiriel continued.

'Since you began running after the lamb, more than fifty years have gone by. We are running to Bethlehem through time, going downhill through history on a diagonal line. It's like running before the wind, or rushing down a moving staircase.'

Elisabet nodded. She wasn't sure she understood everything the angel was saying, but she knew how clever it all was.

'How do you know we're at the beginning of the twentieth century?' The angel raised his arm and pointed at a gold watch on his wrist, decorated with a row of shining pearls. On its face it said 1916.

'It's an angel watch,' he explained. 'It isn't quite as accurate as other watches, but in heaven we're not too particular about all the hours and minutes.'

Now Elisabet understood why the church clock had only struck three even though it had been six or seven o'clock when she ran from the shop, and why the snow had disappeared and it had suddenly become summer. She had run backwards in time.

'You began running along the diagonal path as soon as you started chasing the lamb,' continued the angel Ephiriel. 'That's when the long journey through time and space began.'

Elisabet pointed up at the road.

'There's our lamb again. But look – now there's a grown sheep as well!'

The angel nodded.

'Verily I say unto you, that sheep is going to Bethlehem too.'

With that they began to run. When Elisabet and Ephiriel had caught up with the lamb and the sheep, both of them bounded on as well.

'Lambkin, lambkin!' coaxed Elisabet.

But the lamb and the sheep would not be coaxed into standing still. They were going to Bethlehem, to Bethlehem!

They passed the outskirts of Halden and soon came to a

frontier station. A large signboard announced: 'Frontier. SWEDEN.'

'May I look at your angel watch again?'

Ephiriel stretched out his arm. The watch said 1905.

Then they sped past two frontier guards, the lamb and the sheep first, and Elisabet and the angel Ephiriel just behind them.

'Halt!' shouted the frontier guards. 'In the name of the law!'

But they were already far into Sweden. And they had come a few years closer to the birth of Jesus.

Joachim sat up in bed. So that was why there was a picture of an old car in the Advent calendar! That was why it had suddenly become summer, too.

Joachim was old enough to know that you can't really run backwards in time, but at least you can do it in your thoughts.

At school he had heard that a thousand years to mankind can seem like one single day to God. And the angel Ephiriel had told Elisabet that nothing is impossible for God.

Could Elisabet and the angel really have run backwards in time?

✳ The 4th ✳
✳ of December ✳

WHEN JOACHIM WOKE UP ON FRIDAY, the fourth of December, he made sure it was completely quiet in the house before he opened the fourth door in the calendar.

The picture showed a man in a light blue robe that looked a bit like a nightgown. In his hand he held a tall staff. But Joachim had no time to look at the picture properly, because a scrap of paper fell down into his bed. He unfolded it and read.

 JOSHUA

Elisabet and the angel Ephiriel hurried after the sheep and the lamb. From a rise Ephiriel pointed down at a lake.

'That's the biggest lake in Scandinavia,' he said. 'The watch shows that 1891 years have passed since Jesus was born, but we've only just arrived in Sweden.'

A strongly flowing river ran out of the lake. A bridge arched over the river, and they walked over it to the other side.

'This is the River Göta,' said Ephiriel. 'We'll follow an old cart track along the river bank.'

Before long the sheep and the lamb found pasture that was so green and tempting that it dazzled the eyes.

'Now's our chance,' whispered Elisabet, 'if we go up to them carefully.' But just then a man came walking towards them, wearing a blue tunic and holding a tall staff curved at the top. He said solemnly, 'Peace be with you who walk on the narrow way along the Göta River. My name is Joshua the shepherd.'

'Then you are one of us,' said Ephiriel.

Elisabet didn't understand what the angel meant by that, but then the shepherd said, 'I am coming with you to the Holy Land, for I must be in the fields when the angels announce the glad tidings of the birth of Jesus.'

Then Elisabet had a bright idea.

'If you are a proper shepherd, perhaps you can herd the lamb in this direction.'

The shepherd bowed low. 'That's not difficult for a good shepherd.'

He went over to the sheep and the lamb,
and the next moment the lamb was
kneeling at Elisabet's feet. She knelt
down and stroked its soft fleece.

'I think you must be the fastest
furry animal in the world,' she said, 'but I caught you at last!'

The shepherd thumped his crook on the ground and said,
'To Bethlehem, to Bethlehem!'

The lamb and the sheep bounded away, the shepherd, the
angel and Elisabet after them.

They sped on through Sweden.

✷ The 5th ✷
✷ of December ✷

T HE FIFTH OF DECEMBER was a Saturday. Mama and
Papa usually slept longer on Saturdays. Joachim woke
up at seven as he always did. He sat up in bed and
examined the big picture on the outside of the calendar.

Only now did he discover that one of the shepherds was
holding a crook in his hand – just like Joshua.

Why hadn't he noticed that before?

Every time he looked at the magic calendar he discovered
something new. But surely there couldn't be anything *more*
to see than what had been there all the time? Wouldn't that
be like a conjuring trick? Perhaps that was what made the old
Advent calendar magical? The picture outside had never been
completely finished, but it gradually painted in what was
missing as somebody opened the doors and read the scraps
of paper.

Joachim opened the door with the number 5 on it. Today's

picture was of a rowing boat. In the boat there sat a shepherd, an angel, a little girl and several sheep. Joachim knew who they were, but what interested him most was the little scrap of paper.

He unfolded it and began to read.

 ## THE THIRD SHEEP

Elisabet, the lamb, the angel, the sheep and the shepherd sped through Sweden along dirt roads and grassy cart tracks, between yellow fields and through dense forests until they looked out over a little town by the sea. At the edge of the town stood a large castle.

'We are in Halland,' said the angel Ephiriel. 'The town is called Halmstad. The watch says that 1789 years have passed since Jesus was born.'

Joshua the shepherd said they should hurry on, and they crossed a landscape that became flatter and flatter the further south they came. Between grazing land and enclosed pastures the countryside revealed small villages, each with a little church and a few houses.

They were rushing through dense woodland when Joshua stopped and knelt under a birch tree. He had found a sheep caught in a snare.

'The snare was probably set for a hare or a fox,' he said, loosening a cord from the sheep's leg. 'But now the sheep can come with us to Bethlehem.'

'It's one of us too,' said Ephiriel.

And the sheep seemed to answer. 'Meh!'
it bleated. 'Me-e-eh.'

Off they went again: the lamb and the two
sheep first, the shepherd behind them, Elisabet
and Ephiriel last.

They passed large fields and small villages. Soon they could
glimpse the sea in the distance. In a short while they were
standing on a deserted beach.

'This is Øre Sound,' said Ephiriel. 'My watch shows that
1703 years have passed since Jesus was born. We must get across
to Denmark before the seventeenth century is over.'

'Here's a rowing boat,' announced Joshua.

They climbed on board the boat, the sheep first, Elisabet and
Ephiriel behind them. Joshua pushed the boat out and jumped
on board at the last minute.

The angel Ephiriel rowed, so strongly that the spray foamed
about the prow. Joshua sat in the stern. Suddenly he pointed
forwards and said, 'I can see Denmark.'

'I can see Denmark.'

Joachim thought he could see a little of Denmark too, but it
was only inside his head.

It was extraordinary that Elisabet was able to travel
backwards in time, strange to think that two thousand years
had passed since Jesus was born. But the stories about Jesus had
travelled through those two thousand years so that Joachim had

heard about Him too. In a way Elisabet was travelling in the
other direction.

When Mama and Papa got up they had to see the picture in
the Advent calendar. Joachim pointed to the boat with
Elisabeth, Ephiriel, Joshua and the three sheep, but he had
decided not to talk about the pieces of paper in the calendar.
He had hidden them in the secret box.

✫ The 6th ✫
✫ of December ✫

WHEN JOACHIM WOKE UP on Sunday morning it felt as if he had just fallen asleep, for he hadn't woken once during the whole of that long night.

He was ready to open the sixth door in the Advent calendar. Today there was a picture of a round tower. He would look more closely at the picture afterwards. First he had to read what was on the scrap of paper.

CASPAR

When the boat with Elisabet, the angel Ephiriel, Joshua the shepherd, and the three sheep touched land on the Danish side of the Øre Sound, they were welcomed politely by a black man.

It was Elisabet who discovered him first. The angel, who was rowing, sat with his back to the shore and Joshua was busy keeping the sheep quiet.

'There's a man over there,' she remarked.

The angel glanced over his shoulder and said, 'Then he's one of us.'

The black man had a dark cloak with gold buttons, red woollen trousers, and sheepskin shoes. He came towards them, seized the boat and pulled them up on land. The sheep jumped out first, and soon they were all standing on the beach.

The man with the fine clothes bent down and took Elisabet's hand.

'Greeting to you, my child, and welcome. I am King Caspar of Nubia.'

'Elisabet,' said Elisabet, curtseying politely.

'He's one of the Three Wise Men from the East,' whispered Ephiriel solemnly.

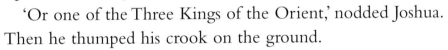

'Or one of the Three Kings of the Orient,' nodded Joshua. Then he thumped his crook on the ground.

'To Bethlehem! To Bethlehem!'

The little procession of pilgrims began to move off again: the three sheep first, Joshua and Caspar the black king next, Elisabet and Ephiriel last.

They leapt along broad cobbled streets, and Ephiriel explained that this was Copenhagen, the King's city. It was so early in the morning that the streets were almost deserted.

Soon they arrived at the very centre of the Danish capital. They stopped in front of a church with a round tower at one end.

'That's the Round Tower which King Christian has just built on to the new Trinity Church,' said Ephiriel. 'The church towers look imposing, but he thought it was a pity that they should stand there to no purpose. So the Round Tower has been built both as a church tower and as a watchtower where astronomers can stand in peace and quiet studying the movements of the planets and the positions of the stars in the sky. These are the days when the first telescopes are being invented.'

The procession of pilgrims began to move along the streets again. Through the city and out to the country they went, between swaying fields of corn and cool, leafy woodland. Denmark seemed to be extra flat: she could see no tall buildings. The only things that pointed upwards occasionally were the churches they passed, all of them built in honour of a little child who once upon a time was born in Bethlehem.

They caught sight of the sea in the distance and came down to a small town called Korsør which lay beside the Great Belt, the broad sound between Sjaelland and Fyn.

The people in the town almost fell over when they caught a glimpse of the astonishing procession, but their terror lasted only a short time, for the next moment the procession had moved one or two weeks backwards in the history of the town. Then there were other people who caught a glimpse of the pilgrimage for a second or two. At that time there was continual talk of angels.

Joshua pointed to a large rowing boat at the water's edge.

'We shall have to borrow that,' he said. 'Hurry up now.

It's nearly 1600 years after Jesus's birth.' And he fell to chasing his sheep on board.

A little later they were out on the Great Belt.

In the evening, when Joachim was going to bed, he tried to push all the open doors shut again so that he could look at the large picture properly. Then it happened again, and this time with one of the Three Wise Men who were kneeling behind the baby Jesus in the manger. His skin was dark, just like Caspar the black king, and Joachim hadn't noticed it before!

★ The 7th ★
★ of December ★

WHEN HE WOKE UP the next morning he opened the seventh door and saw a picture of a sheep eating grass in front of some high walls. He picked up a scrap of paper that was folded over and over, and read what was written on it.

 ### THE FOURTH SHEEP

The angel Ephiriel and the black king Caspar had rowed Elisabet, Joshua, and the three sheep over the Great Belt.

'We're going ashore again,' said Ephiriel. 'This island is called Fyn, and it's exactly 1599 years since Jesus was born in Bethlehem.'

From the sea they ran towards a large castle on a mound between ramparts and ditches. 'That's Nyborg Castle,' the angel told them. 'We're standing in front of the oldest royal fortress in Scandinavia.'

36

Elisabet pointed up at one of the ramparts.
'There's a sheep.'
The angel nodded. 'Then it's one of us.'
With that they all leapt up on to the ramparts,
the three sheep first, Joshua and Caspar after them,
Elisabet and Ephiriel last.

A soldier rushed out from between the
buildings in the castle. He raised a spear
and shouted, 'Sheep thieves!'

When he saw the angel Ephiriel he
threw himself down on the ground.

'Fear not!' said the angel in a
gentle voice. 'I bring you tidings of
great joy. This sheep will come with
us to the Holy Land where the Christ-
child is to be born.'

'Be merciful and take the sheep with you,' the soldier cried.
The sheep in question had already joined the others as if it
belonged to the little flock. Joshua struck his crook against the
rampart and said, 'To Bethlehem! To Bethlehem!'

Off they went across the green island, the four sheep first,
Joshua, Caspar, Ephiriel and Elisabet following them until they
came to a little town beside a narrow strip of water.

'The sound is called the Little Belt,' said Ephiriel. 'The time
is 1504 years after Christ.'

Before Elisabet was able to ask how they were going to cross
the sound, Joshua was on his way towards a boat that lay moored

to a little quay. In the boat sat a young man drawing up a fishing line. When he caught sight of the angel Ephiriel he dropped the line into the sea and threw himself down with his head on the deck.

'Be not afraid,' said Ephiriel. 'We are pilgrims on our way to the Holy Land where Jesus is to be born. Can you row us over the Little Belt?'

'Amen,' replied the ferryman. 'Amen, amen ...'

The angel knew his answer meant yes. The four sheep and the rest of the pilgrims climbed on board the boat.

When they were over on the other side and the sheep began jumping out of the boat, they said thank you and goodbye to the ferryman. As for the ferryman, he only repeated what he had already said over and over again. 'Amen, amen ...'

Joachim had just finished reading what was on the paper when his mother came into the room. He screwed up the paper quickly, but Mama saw that he was hiding something.

'What are you holding in your hand?'

'It's a Christmas present,' he said.

The words 'Christmas present' might have been magic. At any rate they made Mama smile broadly.

'For me?'

Joachim nodded.

'Then I won't look,' said Mama. 'But it must be a very tiny Christmas present.'

'It's infinitely better than nothing,' said Joachim.

Joachim thought that it was strange that everything that had to do with Christmas was so special. It was one of the most secret things in the whole world.

But Mama was mistaken about one thing. What he was holding in his hand wasn't a *tiny* Christmas present.

⋆ The 8th ⋆
⋆ of December ⋆

WHEN JOACHIM CAME HOME from school on the eighth of December a man he did not recognise was standing outside the garden gate.

'Is your name Joachim?' asked the stranger.

Joachim stopped on the path that Papa had almost cleared of snow and turned towards the man. He was quite old; he looked kind too.

'Yes,' he said. 'That's me.'

The man nodded. He came right up to the gate and leaned over it.

'I thought so.' He had rather an odd accent. Perhaps he wasn't Norwegian.

'You've been given a fine Advent calendar, haven't you?'

Joachim gave a start. How did he know that?

'A magic Advent calendar,' answered Joachim.

'A magic Advent calendar, yes. Price: 75 øre. My name's John.

40

I sell flowers at the market.'

Joachim stood stock still. In his Advent calendar he had read about people who had suddenly seen an angel; now it was almost as if he was being visited by an angel himself.

'Did you know there were some pieces of paper in the Advent calendar?' Joachim asked.

'If there's anyone in the whole world who knows, it must be me. Now you know too,' said John.

'Is it home-made?'

'Completely home-made, yes, and very old. But that's an old story too.'

'Did you make the magic Advent calendar?' Joachim asked.

'Yes and no ...'

Joachim was afraid he might go, so he quickly asked another question.

'Did it all really happen, or did you make it up?'

John looked serious. 'It's all right to ask, but it isn't always so easy to answer.'

Joachim said, 'I wondered whether Elisabet in the magic Advent calendar was the same as the Elisabet whose picture was in the bookshop.'

'So the bookseller told you about the old picture?' said John, sighing heavily. 'Well, well, I have nothing to hide any more, I'm too old for that now. But it isn't Christmas yet, so we'd better talk about Elisabet another time.'

He took a step back. 'Sabet ... tebas ...' he mumbled to himself. Joachim didn't understand that, but perhaps he hadn't been meant to hear it.

Finally John said, 'I must go now. But we'll meet again, for that old story links us human beings together.' He walked away rapidly and soon disappeared.

Joachim hurried into the house and opened the door with the number 8 on it. Today there was a picture of a shepherd carrying a lamb on his shoulders. He picked up the paper, smoothed it out carefully, and read.

JACOB

On one of the last days of the year 1499 after Christ four sheep, one shepherd, one King of the Orient, one angel and a little girl from Norway flocked out of a boat that had brought them across the Little Belt to Jutland.

The little procession came to a town at the inner end of a fjord. At one end of the town stood a large fortress.

'This town is called Kolding and is in South Jutland,' said the angel Ephiriel. 'It has been an important trading place for hundreds of years. The fortress is called Koldinghaus and the kings of Denmark have often lived here. The time is 1488 years after Christ's birth.'

Joshua struck the ground with his crook.

'To Bethlehem! To Bethlehem!'

They came to the top of a little ridge with fine views over the countryside. Fresh flowers were growing everywhere, so it must have been early summer. Elisabet pointed down at the ground as she ran.

'Look at all the lovely wild flowers!' she said.

The angel nodded mysteriously.

'They are part of the glory of heaven that has strayed down to earth,' he explained. 'You see, there's so much glory in heaven that it can easily spill over.'

Elisabet pondered over the angel's words and hid them in her heart.

Suddenly the shepherd stopped and pointed at the little flock of sheep.

'A lamb is missing!'

He needed to say no more, for all of them saw that the earth seemed to have swallowed up the lamb with the bell.

'Where is it?' exclaimed Elisabet and she felt her eyes fill with tears. But just then a man appeared over the crest of the ridge. He was wearing clothes exactly like Joshua's and on his shoulders he was carrying the lamb with the bell.

'He is one of us,' said Ephiriel.

The man put the lamb down at Elisabet's feet. He held out his hand to Joshua and said, 'I am Jacob the shepherd and the second of the shepherds in the field. Now I can help care for the flock that's going to Bethlehem.'

Elisabet clapped her hands. Joshua struck the ground with his crook and said, 'To Bethlehem! To Bethlehem!'

The two shepherds ran behind the little flock, with Caspar the black king, the angel Ephiriel and Elisabet behind them.

Joachim stood lost in thought. The angel Ephiriel had said that the wild flowers were a part of the glory of heaven that had strayed down to earth, because there's so much glory in heaven that it can easily spill over. Probably only a flower-seller could write something like that.

J OACHIM COULDN'T STOP THINKING about the words John had muttered to himself. 'Sabet ... Tebas.'

Who or what were Sabet and Tebas? Could these strange words have anything to do with the Advent calendar?

Before he went to bed he wrote the words down in a little notebook so as not to forget them by the morning. Then he discovered something odd: SABET became TEBAS when he read it backwards. So of course TEBAS turned into SABET too.

This was so mysterious that he wrote down the two words like this:

S

A

T E B A S

E

T

Perhaps one day the magic words would help him to understand more about the old Advent calendar.

Suddenly he remembered something the bookseller had said. Hadn't he said that the old flower-seller was a bit odd? Joachim didn't think he seemed the least bit odd. Of course, it was unusual to pour water over people's heads, but it was just the sort of thing that Joachim might suddenly decide to do himself.

As soon as he woke up on the ninth of December he sat up in bed and hurried to open the Advent calendar. It was a picture of a man playing a pipe. After the man came a long procession of children, big and small.

Joachim looked at it for a long time before he picked up the piece of paper that had fallen out of the calendar. He made himself comfortable and read what was on the paper.

 THE FIFTH SHEEP

It was the year 1351 after Christ in the town of Hanover in Germany, immediately after the fearful Plague that had cost so many human lives, not only in Germany, but in the whole of Europe. It was a Monday, and the market stalls on the great market square were about to open. Peasants in their worn, homespun clothes and market women in rough skirts had begun setting out their wares. All of them had lost some of their dear ones. It was just before the dawn of a new day.

It was then that a little flock of sheep suddenly sprang into the market. One of the sheep overturned a table of vegetables.

After the sheep there came a strange company. There were a couple of shepherds, and a man in exotic clothes, black-skinned like an African. The black man was followed by a white-clad figure with wings on its back. Right at the end there appeared a little girl. She stumbled over the shaft of a cart full of cabbages and lay there after the rest of the godly company had left the market.

Elisabet wept bitterly when she saw the angel Ephiriel and all the others disappearing. It was the second time on the long journey south that she had fallen and hurt herself. Now she had lost the procession of pilgrims and was surrounded by people she didn't know. Not only was she in a foreign country, she was in a foreign century too.

The people in the market were terrified by what they had seen. They crowded round Elisabet, and a man poked her with his foot as if he was afraid to touch her. He wrinkled his nose and grunted horribly. But soon an old woman put Elisabet on her feet and tried to comfort her. She spoke a language Elisabet didn't understand.

'I'm going to Bethlehem,' said Elisabet.

And the market woman replied, 'Hamelin? Hamelin?'

'No, no!' sobbed Elisabet. 'To Bethlehem! To Bethlehem!'

The next moment one of the angels of the Lord appeared in an arc of light above the market. Elisabet stretched out her arms towards the angel and cried, 'Ephiriel! Ephiriel!'

The people in the market threw themselves to the ground, but the angel lifted Elisabet up into the air, flew over the spire of the new Market Church, and was gone.

He put her down on a country road outside the town where the sheep, the shepherds, and Caspar the black king were waiting. Joshua struck the ground with his crook. 'To Bethlehem! To Bethlehem!'

After a while they came to a town on the bank of another river.

'This is Hamelin,' said Ephiriel. 'The river is called the Weser, and the year is 1304 after Jesus' birth. A few years ago a dreadful misfortune occurred in this town.'

'What happened?' asked Elisabet.

'The town had been plagued by rats for a long time. But then a rat-catcher arrived in town. He played on a magic pipe, and the sound of the pipe made all the rats follow him. The piper led the rats to the river, where they all drowned.'

'Wasn't that a good thing?'

'Yes, of course, but the people in the town had promised the man a big reward if he could save them from the plague of rats. When he had rid them of the rats, they refused to pay what they owed him.'

'What did the rat-catcher do then?'

'He began to play on his magic pipe again, and all the

48

children in the town were bewitched by the music of the pipe and followed him. They disappeared inside a huge mountain with the piper, and were never seen again.'

Elisabet realised that maybe the woman in the market at Hanover had thought she was one of the children who had been lured into the mountain by the rat-catcher from Hamelin.

They were about to hurry on through Europe and even further back into history, when a sheep came running towards them along the road and joined the others. Now the flock numbered five sheep.

Joshua struck the ground with his crook.

'To Bethlehem! To Bethlehem!'

Joachim found the key to his box and hid the little piece of paper along with all the other pieces.

After school Mama and Joachim went into town to buy an anorak, and Joachim asked to go into the market.

There were not as many people in the market as there were in the summer. Some stallholders were selling wreaths and candles, others were selling all sorts of Christmas presents.

'I wonder how they can bear to stand here in the middle of winter,' shivered Mama. 'There's someone over there selling flowers, too.'

'He's selling flowers in the middle of the winter because the glory of heaven has strayed down to earth,' said Joachim. 'You see, there's so much glory in heaven that it can easily spill over.'

Mama shook her head and sighed in despair. She obviously didn't like him to say such strange things.

John was standing behind a table with lots of flowers on it. He winked at Joachim and gave a little wave.

When they had passed, Joachim turned round. John was pretending to play on an invisible pipe.

T HE NEXT DAY JOACHIM WOKE UP and opened the tenth
door in the magic Advent calendar. Today there was a
picture of an angel at the top of a church tower. Out
of the calendar fell a scrap of paper, folded over and over.
Joachim unfolded it and began to read.

 IMPURIEL

It happened at Paderborn at the end of the thirteenth century.
Into the little town halfway between Hanover and Cologne
rushed a frisky flock of sheep, followed by two shepherds, a black
king, a little girl and an angel with wings outspread.

It was early in the morning before the town was awake;
only a night watchman was out in the streets. He called out
sternly to the two shepherds who were chasing their flock of
sheep through the town. The next moment he caught sight of

the angel hovering above the cobblestones. Then he raised his arms to the sunrise and exclaimed, 'Allelulia! Allelulia!'

Whereupon he retreated round a corner and left the streets to the godly procession.

They stopped in front of a church in the middle of the town.

'That's St Bartholomew's Church,' said Ephiriel. 'It was built in the eleventh century and is called after one of Jesus's twelve apostles.'

Elisabet had noticed something strange. She pointed up at the spire on the church tower.

'There's a white bird sitting up there,' she said.

Ephiriel smiled. 'If only there were,' he said.

A few seconds later, what Elisabet had thought was a bird took off and flew down in a spiral towards the pilgrims. She realised that the bird wasn't a bird after all. What had been sitting on the church spire was an angel. But it was not a grown angel: it was no larger than she was herself.

The child angel alighted at Elisabet's feet.

'Wonderful!' he exclaimed. 'My name is Impuriel and I'm coming with you to Bethlehem.'

He whirled around a bit, peered up at Caspar and the two shepherds, then looked up at Ephiriel and said, 'I've been waiting for a quarter of an eternity.'

Caspar stood thinking. It was obvious he had something on his mind.

'A quarter of an eternity,' he began. 'It's not easy to say how long a quarter of an eternity lasts. First you have to find out how long a *whole* eternity lasts, then you have to divide it by four, but exactly how long a whole eternity lasts is very difficult to calculate. No matter which number you start with, eternity will last even longer. Calculating whole or half eternities is a matter for heaven alone.'

The angel Impuriel looked offended. 'But I've been sitting on top of the church tower for *hours*,' he said.

'Very possibly, but that's not the same as sitting there for a quarter of an eternity,' said Caspar.

To avoid a quarrel and not just a quarter of a quarrel, Joshua struck the cobblestones with his crook, and said, 'To Bethlehem! To Bethlehem!'

They set off through the town and out along roads and cattle trails. Impuriel sprang in front of the five sheep, so the pilgrimage was guarded by angels at both ends.

They saw many towns and villages, but didn't stop until they came to the old Roman colonial city of Cologne on the bank of the River Rhine.

'Angel-time says it's 1272 years after Christ,' said Ephiriel. 'They've begun building the great cathedral of Cologne, but it won't be finished for hundreds of years.'

And they hurried along the bank of the biggest river Elisabet had ever seen.

Impuriel said, 'Glorious countryside isn't it? We're going up the Rhine Valley. There are fortresses and castles, steep vineyards and Gothic cathedrals, dandelions and rhubarb.'

They hurried along the bank of the biggest river Elisabet had ever seen. The valley became narrower and narrower and the mountains higher and higher. They ran past small towns and villages. Out on the river floated an occasional barge.

As they sped through the landscape, Elisabet asked Ephiriel whether he had met Impuriel before.

'All the angels in heaven have known each other through all eternity,' said Ephiriel, laughing.

'Are there an awful lot of you?'

'Yes, a whole host.'

'How can you all know each other, then?'

'We've had the whole of eternity to get to know each other, and you see, that's a very long time.

'Do all the angels have different names?'

'Of course. Otherwise we couldn't call out to each other. Otherwise we wouldn't have been *persons* either.'

And Ephiriel began to say all the angel names, one after the other.

'The angels in heaven are called Ariel, Beriel, Curruciel,

Daniel, Ephiriel, Fabiel, Gabriel, Hammarubiel, Immanuel, Joachiel, Chachaduriel, Luxuriel, Michael, Narriel ... '

'That's enough!' said Elisabet. 'I think it's very clever to think up so many different names all ending in -el.'

Ephiriel nodded. 'God's imagination is infinite, just as there are infinitely many stars in the sky. No angel is exactly like another, nor are humans either. You can make a thousand identical machines, but they are so easy to make that even a human can do it.'

Finally Ephiriel spoke some words that Elisabet hid in her heart. 'Every person on this earth is a unique work of creation.'

Joachim hid the little piece of paper in his secret box as usual and placed it under his pillow.

When he came home from school in the afternoon, Mama was there. She had opened the secret box! On the dining table lay all ten pieces of paper that Joachim had found in the magic Advent calendar. He was furious.

'That's *my* secret box and you should never have opened it!' he cried. He rushed into his bedroom and slammed the door behind him as hard as he could.

Joachim sat on his bed and tried to look up at the magic Advent calendar, but his eyes were so wet that the colours slid into one another, and he could no longer pick out the angels from the shepherds in the fields. *Everything* was spoilt. The Advent calendar had suddenly become ordinary, like every

other Advent calendar. It wasn't
the least bit magical any more.

After a long time something began
to sing in his ears, and the song he heard was something
like: SABET-TEBAS-SABET-TEBAS-SABET-TEBAS …

It was such a mysterious song that he suddenly
realised that perhaps it didn't make any difference
whether Mama and Papa knew about the scraps of
paper in the Advent calendar. Perhaps the magic Advent
calendar was so full of secrets that there would be enough
for the whole family.

There was a knock at the door. Joachim didn't answer, but
after a little while Mama cautiously opened the door.

'Can you forgive me?' asked Mama.

'Did you read what was on the secret pieces of paper?' asked
Joachim.

'I suppose I did,' said Mama. 'But you see I don't know
which piece came out of the calendar first. Maybe you can
show me – and perhaps read it all to Papa?'

Joachim considered carefully.

'All right, then.'

He was a little relieved at what had happened, really. From
now on he had no need to hide anything. Besides, he would be
able to ask Mama and Papa if there was something he didn't
understand.

From now on the magic Advent calendar would belong to
the whole family.

The 11th *of December*

W HEN IT WAS EVENING and Joachim had to go to bed, he sat up for a long time, staring at the calendar.

IT HAD HAPPENED AGAIN! On the big calendar picture were painted many angels floating down from the sky. Joachim had seen that before. But only today did he discover that one of the angels in the picture was a cherub.

He was quite sure. Impuriel the cherub had not been in the picture until Joachim had read that he flew in spirals down from the tall church tower.

The next morning Joachim opened the eleventh door in the Advent calendar. He had to coax the piece of paper out before he discovered a picture of a horse and rider. He made himself comfortable under the duvet and read what was on the sheet of paper.

BALTHAZAR

Five sheep, two shepherds, two angels, one King of Orient, and a little girl from Norway were speeding up the Valley of the Rhine 1199 years after Jesus was born. They could just glimpse a church tower on the other side of the river. Ephiriel told them it was Mainz Cathedral.

'We have to cross the river,' said Joshua. 'It's a pity, because we shall have to frighten another poor ferryman and explain that we're pilgrims on our way to the Holy Land.'

'We shall have to try to do it gently,' said Ephiriel.

'I can see a boat down there,' exclaimed Impuriel.

He flew high in the air, beating his short wings in the direction of the boat, with the rest of the procession after him, and started talking to a man who was sitting on the river bank.

'Can you row us across? We're going all the way to Bethlehem, and we don't have much time if we're to get there before Jesus is born. We're on a godly errand, you see, so we're not just anybody.'

Ephiriel hurried after him. When he had caught up with Impuriel he nodded apologetically at the ferryman and said to Impuriel, 'How many times do I have to remind you that first of all you must say, "Fear not"?'

But the ferryman, who was unusually and splendidly dressed in a long red cloak, was not scared by the cherub. He turned to Ephiriel and said, 'My name is Balthazar, Second Wise Man and

King of Sheba. I'm going the same way as you.'

'Then you are one of us,' said Ephiriel.

The two Wise Men embraced each other.

'It's been a very long time,' said the one.

'And it was a very, very long way from the Rhine,' answered the other.

'But it's very, very, very pleasant to see you again.'

They had their arms round each other, so it was not easy to say who had said what. But now the whole of the pilgrims' procession went on board the boat. The Kings of Orient each took an oar and rowed across the river, which was almost as wide as a stretch of ocean.

The pilgrims hurried along the west bank of the Rhine.

When they tumbled into the town of Worms in the year of Our Lord 1162, they met a rider on horseback – a soldier who had been out on night duty, perhaps. The angel Impuriel flew over to the man, buzzed round him like an excited bumble bee, and repeated 'Fear not! Fear not! Fear not!'

The poor man was extremely scared. He spurred on his horse and galloped away round some low buildings. He didn't even have time to say 'Alleluia' or 'God be praised'.

'You only need to say it once,' Ephiriel chided Impuriel, 'but you must say it in a gentle, soft, heavenly voice. "Fe-ear no-ot!" you must say. It's a good idea to keep your arms down too, to show you're not carrying a weapon.'

Balthazar the Wise Man pointed up at a cathedral with six towers.

'Everywhere and at all times people have stretched their arms out to God,' he said. 'The church towers point up to heaven too, but they last much longer.'

The shepherds bent their heads respectfully at these wise words, and Elisabet felt she had to repeat them to herself before she was quite certain what he meant.

In the city of Basle on the southern bank of the Rhine they stopped in front of another big cathedral.

'The time tells us that 1119 years have passed since the Christ-child was born,' announced Ephiriel. 'This cathedral with five naves has just celebrated its centenary. But for hundreds of years Basle has been an important crossroads for travellers who have journeyed through the Alps between Italy and Northern Europe. We are going to follow the same route over the St Bernard Pass.'

'To Bethlehem!' said Joshua the shepherd, striking his crook on the ground. 'To Bethlehem!'

Whereupon they set off upwards through the Swiss mountains.

Joachim sat in bed, thinking about the strange pilgrimage to Bethlehem. After a while his mother and father came in to read what was on the piece of paper.

'We took home a small miracle from the bookshop, didn't we, Joachim?' said Papa. 'Can you imagine how it was made?'

'I think John made it,' said Joachim.

'The bookseller said something about someone called John, didn't he?'

Joachim wondered whether he ought to tell Mama and Papa that he had met John. But he didn't. He had to keep *one* little secret for himself. Because there was something else as well: SABET … TEBAS … SABET … TEBAS.

'If this calendar was made by a flower-seller,' said Papa, 'he's certainly inventive.'

Mama agreed. 'Yes, he has plenty of imagination.'

Joachim shook his head.

'He may not have so much imagination if the whole story is true.'

Papa laughed. 'You surely don't think you really can run all the way to Bethlehem and far back in time as well?'

'Nothing is impossible for God,' said Joachim.

Suddenly Mama gave a little gasp.

'Do you remember that old story from way back?' she said to Papa. 'There really was a little girl who disappeared from this town while she and her mother were out doing their Christmas shopping. I think *she* was called Elisabet.'

Papa nodded. 'It was some time after the war. *Was* she called Elisabet?'

'I think so,' said Mama, 'but I'm not sure.'

Suddenly it was as if Mama and Papa had forgotten Joachim,

they were so busy talking to each other.

'So maybe he's remembered that old story and made up the rest himself,' suggested Papa. 'If it *is* this flower-seller who's made it.'

'Can you find out whether she was called Elisabet?' said Joachim.

'Yes, I should think so,' replied Papa. 'Not that it really matters what she was called.'

'I think it matters a lot,' Joachim said. 'Because the lady in the photo was called Elisabet too.'

The 12th of December

WHEN PAPA CAME HOME FROM WORK on the
eleventh of December Mama and Joachim were
waiting for him.

'Have you found out what she was called?' asked Joachim.

'Yes, she was called Elisabet. Elisabet Hansen, in fact. It
happened in December 1948.'

Dinner was ready, so they sat down at the table.

'I went into the bookshop as well,' continued Papa. 'I went
into the storeroom with him, and there he found the photo
that the flower-seller had once put in his window in exchange
for a glass of water. I have it in my briefcase.'

'Then fetch it,' said Mama.

So he did. He put the picture on the table. Joachim snatched
it and Mama leaned over it.

Elisabet —

It showed a young woman with long fair hair. Round her neck she was wearing a silver cross set with a red stone. She was leaning against a small car. At the top of the photo was a large dome. At the bottom was written 'Elisabet'.

'Hm, no last name,' said Papa. 'It's not exactly an unusual name, but it's written in Norwegian. In many countries Elisabet is spelt differently.'

'Do you think she's not Norwegian, then?' asked Mama.

'No idea,' said Papa. 'But look at the photo carefully. The dome in the background is St Peter's in Rome. She's standing in the road that leads to St Peter's Square. The car dates from the end of the fifties.'

'I feel almost scared,' whispered Mama. 'What are we getting mixed up in?'

When Joachim woke up on the twelfth of December Mama and Papa were in his room before he had managed to open his eyes. That was a bit special because it was Saturday, when he was usually up long before the others.

'*You* must open the calendar,' said Papa. 'Hurry up!'

The picture was of a man in a red tunic, holding a large sign. Mama and Papa sat on the bed. Joachim had picked up a little piece of paper, folded over and over. He smoothed it out and read aloud what was written on the paper in very tiny writing.

QUIRINIUS

The five sheep had crossed a ridge and begun to run down into a fertile agricultural district. Impuriel fluttered round the little flock, and after the sheep and the cherub came Jacob and Joshua, Caspar and Balthazar, Ephiriel and Elisabet.

They passed several lakes. The biggest and most beautiful was Lake Geneva. It glittered so that it looked as if a piece of heaven had fallen down to earth. Only when Elisabet looked up and saw that there was no hole in the sky was she able to be quite sure that the picture of the sky in the big lake was only a reflection.

Again they ran along an old road alongside a river in a deep valley. Ephiriel told them that the river was called the Rhône and that all the water it carried with it from the Alps ran down first into Lake Geneva, and later right down to the Mediterranean.

They ran across an old bridge to the
other side of the river and stopped in front
of a monastery. There were high Alps on
every side with snow on their peaks.

'To Bethlehem!' called Joshua, and
they sped upwards towards the
mountains. The air was so thin and clear
that Elisabet thought she must be on the
way to heaven.

At the top of the mountain pass stood a large house.

'The time is 1045 years after Christ,' said the angel Ephiriel.
'That house is a hospice whose purpose is to look after people
who are crossing the Alps. It's brand new and has been built by
Bernard of Menton. From now on and for the rest of time the
Benedictine monks will live up here and organise a rescue
service for people who are lost in the mountains. They are
helped by their clever St Bernard dogs.'

'Right!' said the cherub Impuriel. 'For Jesus wanted to teach
humans to help one another when they were in distress. Once
he told a story about a man who was on his way from Jerusalem
to Jericho, and was attacked by robbers who left him half dead at
the side of the road. Several priests passed by, but none of them
bent down to help the poor man, though he was in danger of
losing his life. Jesus thought there wasn't much point in being
priests if they couldn't even be bothered to help a fellow human
being in distress. They might just as well forget all their prayers.'

Elisabet nodded, and Impuriel continued, 'But then a

Samaritan came past, and Samaritans were not very popular in Judea, because their religion was a bit different from that of the Jews. But the Samaritan had compassion on him and helped the unfortunate man so that he saved his life. Yes indeed! For there's no sense in believing what's right unless it leads to helping people in distress.'

Elisabet nodded again and hid the cherub's words in her heart.

At one point where the pass forked a man was standing with a large sign in his hand. He was wearing a long red tunic. If he had not moved, one might have thought he was a petrified Roman from the Roman Empire.

On the sign was written 'TO BETHLEHEM' in capital letters. An arrow had been drawn in as well, to show which path they should follow.

'A living road sign!' exclaimed Elisabet.

Ephiriel nodded. 'Verily I say unto you, that road sign must be one of us.'

The man with the sign took a step towards Elisabet, offered her his hand and said, 'Congrat … no, no, that wasn't quite correct. I mean, at your service, my friends! The very first thing I must remember to do is to say my name because I, too, have been allowed to take part in this Advent calendar. My name is Quirinius, Governor of Syria … attractive appearance, closer acquaintance desired … well, well, the most important thing is, of course, to be good and kind. Dixi!'

Elisabet couldn't help laughing; he talked so oddly. It was as if there were two people talking at once, for he interrupted himself the whole time. He handed her the sign. He had perhaps been standing and holding it for an eternity with the wind flapping in his tunic. He said, 'And this … I am asking for your attention, my friends … for here I have the actual prize … I ought to say that this prize is for you. Dixi!'

'Am I to have the sign?' said Elisabet in astonishment.

And Quirinius replied, 'Only on the one side … I mean you must turn it right round, you understand. Dixi!'

Elisabet didn't understand why he said Dixi all the time, but the angel Ephiriel whispered that 'dixi' was Latin and meant that he had finished speaking.

Elisabet turned the sign round and saw to her great surprise that what she was holding in her hand was an Advent calendar with twenty-four doors to be opened. Above each door was painted a picture of a young woman with fair hair. She was standing in front of a church with a large dome on top.

'The first twelve,' said Quirinius. 'You may open the first twelve doors, for we've come exactly so far on our journey. Dixi!'

Elisabet sat down on a rock and opened the first door. Behind it was a picture of a lamb. Behind the next door was an angel and behind the third a sheep. Then there followed pictures of a shepherd, another sheep, a King of Orient, a sheep, a shepherd, a sheep, a cherub, and another King of Orient. Elisabet saw that they were pictures of everyone who had joined the pilgrimage on its long way through Europe.

'Thank you very much!' she said.

'But you haven't opened the twelfth door,' said Ephiriel. Elisabet opened the twelfth door as well, and now she was looking down at a tiny picture of a fair-haired woman in front of the big dome of a church.

Joshua struck his shepherd's crook against a cairn. 'To Bethlehem! To Bethlehem!'

They sat looking at each other. Then Joachim began to laugh. 'I hope Quirinius is going all the way to Bethlehem with them,' he said.

Mama and Papa went on examining the piece of paper. 'He's brought the young woman into the story of little Elisabet today,' said Papa.

'And then, he's made another little Advent calendar inside the big one,' said Mama.

Papa nodded. 'Of course he must have meant something by it.'

'Do you think there's yet another calendar inside the little Advent calendar?' asked Joachim.

'Who knows?' said Mama. 'Who knows?'

The 13th of December

WHEN JOACHIM WOKE on the thirteenth of December his mother and father were in his room already. Joachim knew they were as curious as he was to see what was in the Advent calendar.

'*You* get to open it, my lad,' said Papa.

Joachim sat up and fished out the folded piece of paper. The picture in the calendar showed a rainbow.

He sat in bed with Mama on one side of him and Papa on the other. They both leaned over him while Mama read what was on the sheet of paper.

 THE SIXTH SHEEP

A little procession was running down the steep mountains in the Alps from the St Bernard Pass. They spent only half a second in each place, for they were running, not just down the steep slopes towards Val d'Aosta in Northern Italy – they were speeding down through history too.

So a party of monks, who were on their way up from Val d'Aosta one day in June, in the year 998, saw them for only a short moment – just as lightning sweeps across the sky, pouring out a flood of light over the landscape for a second or two.

'Look!' exclaimed one of the monks.

'What?' asked the other.

'I thought I saw a strange procession on its way down through the valley. There were people and animals. Behind them all ran a little girl with an angel.'

The third monk agreed. 'I saw them too. It was like a heavenly host.'

The monk who had seen nothing shook his head in disbelief.

Four years earlier a party of merchants from Milan had seen the same as the two monks. That had been a few kilometres further down the valley.

The godly throng stopped for a little while to enjoy the

view over the beautiful Val d'Aosta. Ephiriel pointed up at Mont Blanc and the sharp peak of the Matterhorn. Elisabet was more interested in studying the Advent calendar she had been given by the Governor of Syria.

She pointed at opening number twelve where there was a picture of an Advent calendar exactly the same as the one she had in her hand, turned to Quirinius and asked, 'Can I open the doors in the tiny little calendar as well?'

Quirinius shook his head. 'Unfortunately not. That calendar is sealed with seven seals. Dixi!'

'We are such Wise Men that we can reveal what is inside it, all the same,' said Caspar the first Wise Man. 'Something mysterious is written there in tiny little letters.'

'Tell me, then!' said Elisabet.

'Behind the first door is written Elisabet,' Caspar began. 'Behind the second is written Lisabet, and behind the third Isabet. Then come Sabet, Abet, Bet and Et. That's the first seven doors.'

'And what then?' said Elisabet, with a broad smile.

Balthazar, the second Wise Man, replied, 'After that come Te, Teb, Teba, Tebas, Tebasi, Tebasil and Tebasile. Then there are only ten doors left.'

'What's behind them?'

'Elisabet, Lisabet, Isabet, Sabet, Abet, Bet and Et.'

'But then there are still three doors left,' said Elisabet.

Caspar nodded solemnly. 'Behind door number 22 is written Roma, behind door number 23 is written Amor, and behind door number 24 the name Jesus is written in very beautiful and artistic lettering. One letter is red, the second is orange, the third is yellow, the fourth blue, and the fifth violet. Altogether that makes all the colours of the rainbow. Jesus was like a whole rainbow.'

'Why?'

'When it's been raining heavily, and the sun breaks through the dark clouds, the rainbow appears in the sky. It's as if a little bit of Jesus is in the air, for Jesus was a rainbow between heaven and earth.'

Joshua lifted up his shepherd's crook and struck a stone with such force that it echoed all round the mountains.

'To Bethlehem!' he said. 'To Bethlehem!'

And it was as if the mountains replied, 'Lehem, Lehem, Lehem …'

It didn't take long for them to reach the Valley of the Po. That is the name of the fertile country that lies around the great River Po, which flows from the Italian Alps in the west to the Adriatic Sea in the east. Ephiriel told them they would be going the same way as the river.

They travelled through the countryside until the River Po met another big river called the Ticino, near the trading city of Pavia. Ephiriel told them that the angel watch showed 904 and that Pavia already had a university that was famous throughout Europe.

Jacob the shepherd pointed down at a large raft that was lying by the river bank and said, 'We'll borrow that.'

So the whole of the long procession of pilgrims jumped on board the raft.

As they were about to push off from the bank, a man came running towards them with a sheep in his arms.

'Accept my sincere offering!' he said.

So six sheep had to be crammed together on the narrow raft.

When they were out on the river, Quirinius said that Elisabet could open door number 13 in the Advent calendar. Behind it was a picture of a man carrying a sheep.

When Mama had finished reading, the family sat on the bed for a long time without saying anything.

'Lehem, Lehem, Lehem!' said Mama at last, almost as if she were singing it.

'Sabet … Tebas,' said Joachim.

He surprised himself. There it was again! John had in fact mumbled half Elisabet's name. And he'd never thought of it before! Then he had said the same half of her name backwards.

But why had he done that?

Papa had something to say too.

'If only I could find this flower-seller maybe we'd find the answer to how the Advent calendar was made. Or why, as far as that goes.'

Joachim could no longer manage to keep his meeting with John secret. It was as if this last little secret was exploding inside his head, so it was good to let it out.

'John was at the gate one day when I came home from school,' he said. 'He got our address from the man in the bookshop.'

'And you didn't tell us?' said Papa.

'I didn't think it was important. He only wanted to know who I was.'

'Yes, yes. But what did he tell you?' said Papa impatiently. 'He must have said something about the magic Advent calendar?'

'He said it wasn't Christmas yet. Then he said he'd tell me more about Elisabet another time.'

All that afternoon Joachim repeated two names inside himself: Elisabet … Tebasile … Elisabet.

One name was like a reflection of the other. But when Joachim looked at himself in the mirror, he saw himself, even though the picture in the mirror was reversed.

Could it all be a secret message that the two Elisabets were one and the same person? But Tebasile sounded like a proper name too.

Could there be someone called Tebasile as well?

That evening Joachim lay for a long time staring at the ceiling before he could relax. In the end he had to get up and write something in his little notebook. It was something he had seen inside his head.

He wrote:

```
S A B E T
A       E
B       B
E       A
T E B A S
```

The 14th of December

THE NEXT DAY JOACHIM WOKE UP before Mama and Papa. He sat up in bed. Only ten days left till Christmas Eve.

What was going to happen to Elisabet, the angel Ephiriel, and all the others who were going to Bethlehem?

Before he managed to open the Advent calendar, Mama and Papa were in his room.

'Let's get going,' said Papa.

Joachim opened the door with the number 14 on it. The folded piece of paper fell down into the bed, and they saw a picture of a raft with people, animals and angels on it.

They sat on the edge of the bed. That day it was Joachim's turn to read.

77

ISAAC

Towards the end of the ninth century a strange raft was sailing on the River Po in the direction of the Adriatic Sea to the east. The country they were sailing through was called Lombardy. On the raft stood a small flock of sheep, bleating crossly because they were not allowed to drink the river water. The smallest sheep was scuttling to and fro, so that a little bell hanging round its woolly neck was tinkling.

Two Wise Men were pointing at objects around them, and saying wise words about the beautiful country they were sailing through.

At the back of the raft stood a man in Roman clothes, steering with a long oar. Such clothes had not long been out of fashion. He was talking to a small girl who was holding a piece of cardboard in her hands. On one side was written, 'TO BETHLEHEM'; on the other was a picture of a young woman with long fair hair.

Most conspicuous were two angels standing forward on the raft, beating their wings to stop the boat drifting towards the river bank.

Now and again the cherub Impuriel turned to the others and praised the beauty of the landscape.

Once or twice somebody on the shore noticed them. But the raft was revealed for only a brief second. That's because it wasn't just sailing down the Valley of the Po, it was sailing down through history too. When a little child stood on the bank of the river and pointed at the strange raft, it disappeared even before the child's forefinger had time to unfold.

They passed old Roman bridges and buildings, theatres, temples and aqueducts.

Before long Joshua pointed at the river bank. 'We'll land over there.'

All the pilgrims alighted from the raft, those on two legs, those on four, and those with wings on their shoulders. They passed a country church and turned uphill through the countryside.

The towns were not very large at this period, but soon they were approaching one of the largest. Ephiriel told them it was called Padua.

Just before they sped through the town gate they caught sight of a man in a blue tunic. He was sitting on a stone with his head in his hands. It looked as if he had been sitting there for a very long time.

Impuriel flew towards him, hovered in the air right in front of him, fluttering his wings, and said, 'Fear not and be in no wise afraid. I am Impuriel and am one of God's angels who is out on a sacred errand.'

It looked as if the cherub's words had an effect, for the man did not throw himself to the ground and did not hide his head. He said neither 'Alleluia' nor 'Gloria Dei'. He simply got to his feet and walked towards them.

'Then he is one of us,' said Ephiriel.

The man offered his hand to Elisabet.

'I am Isaac the shepherd and I am going the same way as you.'

That made it much easier to guide the six sheep through Padua.

Outside the town walls they stopped in front of a small monastery.

'Strange to see a Roman town again,' said Quirinius. 'I wonder who's the emperor now.'

Ephiriel looked at his angel watch.

'It's exactly 800 years after Christ. On Christmas Day this year Charles the Great will be crowned Emperor of Rome.'

'Then we'll soon be starting on a new century,' said Joshua. He struck his shepherd's crook against the monastery wall.

'To Bethlehem! To Bethlehem!'

The 15th of December

WHEN JOACHIM WOKE UP on the fifteenth of December there were only ten doors left to open in the magic Advent calendar. He didn't even have time to sit up in bed before Mama and Papa were in his room.

'Let's get going,' said Papa.

Joachim pulled himself up in bed and opened door number 15. He had to fish out the scrap of folded paper and be careful so that it didn't tear. The picture showed islands and skerries with houses on them; the small islands were bathed in radiant sunshine.

That day it was Papa's turn to read. He grabbed the piece of paper, cleared his throat, and read loudly and clearly from the fragile sheet.

 THE SEVENTH SHEEP

The pilgrims came to the Venetian lagoon at the top of the Adriatic Sea.

They paused on a little rise with a view over the lagoon, and Ephiriel started to point out all the islands and skerries that studded the water. On many of the islets the Venetians had built houses, on some of them churches as well. Several of the islets were so close together that bridges had been built between them. Everywhere there were scores of small fishing boats.

'The time is 797 years after Christ,' announced Ephiriel. 'We see the young Venice, which will soon be the name of the 118 islands. The Venetians settled here in order to be protected from the sea pirates and barbarians who were roving about.'

'I can't see any gondolas,' complained Elisabet.

Ephiriel laughed. 'But you're not in the Venice of the twentieth century. I said the time was 797, and that people had lived here for only a couple of centuries. Venice will soon become so thickly populated that one island will scarcely be separated from another.'

While they stood looking out over all the small islets and islands, a rowing boat came past. One end was filled with salt. In the other end stood some sheep, bleating at the sun which was about to break through the morning mist.

The man who was rowing the boat was so frightened when he caught sight of the procession of pilgrims that he covered his eyes with his arm, took a step backwards, and lost his balance so that he fell head over heels into the water. Elisabet saw him come to the surface a few seconds later and then go under again.

'He's drowning!' she cried. 'We must save him.'

But the angel Ephiriel was already on his way. He hovered gracefully above the glittering water, seized the man when he surfaced again and lifted him up on land, dripping wet. Ephiriel drew in the rowing boat.

The man lay down on the ground and coughed fit to burst his lungs. He gasped for breath and said, 'Gratie, gratie …'

Elisabet tried to explain that they were on their way to Bethlehem to greet the Christ-child and that he needn't be frightened. Impuriel had begun circling round him.

'Fear not,' he said, in a voice as soft as silk, 'and be in no wise afraid. But you should not have been all alone on the sea if you can't swim, for you can't always expect an angel to be around to save you. We wander about only very rarely, you know.'

It didn't look as if Impuriel's advice was any comfort to the man, but the cherub sat down beside him, patted him on the cheek, and went on repeating 'Fear not'. It must have had an effect, for the man got to his feet and trudged back to his boat. He lifted a little lamb out of it and walked back towards them.

'Agnus Dei,' he said.

That means 'God's Lamb', and the lamb joined the rest of the flock of sheep without protest. Joshua struck his shepherd's crook

on the ground and said, 'To Bethlehem! To Bethlehem!' and
they sprang off again.

At the very end of the Venetian Gulf stood the old Roman
town of Aquilela. As they ran, Ephiriel pointed to a monastery.

'The time is 718 years after Christ. But there have been
Christian communities here from ancient times.'

The procession of pilgrims sped on through the town of
Trieste. Then they continued south, across country, through
Croatia.

That day Mama met Joachim at school, and they took the bus to
town to meet Papa and have a pizza. From the pizza restaurant
they could look down on the market in front of the cathedral.

As they ate Papa kept asking, 'Can you see the flower-seller,
Joachim?' and every time Joachim had to answer no. John
wasn't at the market selling flowers any more.

They bought some chunky candles and a couple of
Christmas presents, then went into the bookshop where
Joachim had found the magic Advent calendar.

The bookseller recognised Papa and Joachim at once, and
shook Mama's hand too.

'Here we are again,' said Papa. 'We wondered whether you
had seen anything of this remarkable flower-seller.'

The bookseller shook his head. 'It's quite a while since he
was here. He's not usually around much at this time of year.'

'The magic Advent calendar is a bit of a mystery,' explained

Mama. 'We wanted to invite him home to us, to thank him for it properly.'

They agreed that the bookseller should ask John to phone them.

'Just one more thing,' said Papa as they were leaving. 'Do you know what country he comes from?'

'I think he said he was born in Damascus,' said the bookseller.

When they were in the car going home, Papa sat drumming his fingers on the steering wheel. 'If only we had found that man!' he said.

'At least we found out where he comes from,' replied Mama. 'Isn't Damascus the capital of Syria?'

FOR THE REST OF THE EVENING they talked about Elisabet, John, and the magic Advent calendar. Even when nobody said anything, they all knew what the others were thinking about.

Joachim had put the photo of the grown-up Elisabet on the mantelpiece. He would suddenly look up from the television to the old photograph and say, 'Maybe she was his girlfriend.'

Mama and Papa heard what he said. Papa put a cup on the coffee table. 'Yes, maybe.'

'Because inside that tiny little Advent calendar,' continued Mama, 'the one inside the Advent calendar that Quirinius gave Elisabet, was written, not just Elisabet and Tebasile. There was Roma and Amor as well. Amor means love.'

'But that's Roma backwards,' said Joachim. 'So perhaps Tebasile really means something as well.'

Early on the morning of the sixteenth of December Mama and Papa came in to Joachim and woke him up.

Joachim rubbed sleep out of his eyes and found the door with the number 16 on it. The folded sheet of paper fell out on to the bed, but Papa picked it up quickly. Behind the door was a picture of an old castle.

'I'll read it,' said Mama. It was her turn that day.

They made themselves comfortable.

DANIEL

It happened in the days when the old Roman Empire was divided into two. In both East and West the Christian religion had taken root in the people, but the Christian world was still being plundered by heathen peoples. They delayed the building of new churches, stole gold and silver, and pillaged whole cities.

A decree was sent out from the Pope in Rome that the Church's property should be defended against the foreign races who had not yet heard about Jesus. That was when a strange procession advanced through time and space on its way to Bethlehem, the city of David. They came from a distant future.

At Salonae in Dalmatia they stopped in front of the ancient ruins of a Roman imperial palace. At first the ruins seemed abandoned, but the godly company entered by way of a small gate in the wall and discovered that they were teeming with people. It was like tearing the bark away from an old log to see insects creeping inside.

When the angel Ephiriel saw all the people in the town he said, 'The angel watch says 688 years after Christ. We are standing inside the walls of the palace of the Emperor Diocletian. Diocletian was born in this part of the country about 250 years after Christ. He fought against the nomadic tribes and tried to rebuild the old Roman Empire. He closed the Christian churches and started to persecute the Christians cruelly. When he died he was buried here in the great palace. But only a few years after his death the whole of the Roman Empire became Christian. A complete town grew up inside the old palace. Much later this town will be called Split.'

Joshua struck his shepherd's crook against the old town wall and said, 'To Bethlehem! To Bethlehem!'

They hurried on down through Dalmatia. They sprang over hills and ridges and often had good views of the Adriatic Sea.

On a rise with a view over the sea they met another shepherd, who was sitting under a pine tree to protect himself from the strong sun. He had the same light blue tunic as Joshua, Jacob and Isaac. When he saw the procession of pilgrims approaching, he got to his feet and came to meet them.

'Glory to God in the highest,' he said. 'My name is Daniel and I have been waiting here for many years, but I knew you would pass through Dalmatia some time during the seventh century. I am coming with you to Bethlehem.'

'Yes, indeed!' said Impuriel the cherub. 'For you are one of us.'

Soon they came to a lake. At the end of the lake was a town.

'This is the Lake of Scodra,' said Ephiriel. 'After many centuries this land will be called Albania. The angel watch shows that 602 years have passed since Jesus was born. At this time, and throughout the Middle Ages, the Christian church had two different capitals. The one is Rome, and the other is Byzantium at the entrance to the Black Sea.'

'But didn't they believe the same things?'

'On the whole, yes, but they showed it in slightly different ways. People have come and gone, and church traditions and services have come and gone too, even though the start of it all was something that happened one Christmas night in Bethlehem, the city of David.'

Impuriel ruffles his wings and said, 'Yes, indeed! For there was only one Mary and only one Christ-child. Since then many millions of images of Mary and the Christ-child have been painted and fashioned, and none of them are alike.'

Elisabet hid these words in her heart. But Impuriel beat his wings and came right up to her.

'God created only one Adam and one Eve. They were children who played hide-and-seek and climbed the trees in the Garden of Eden. But these two children ate the fruit of the Tree of Knowledge, and then they grew up. Soon Adam and Eve had children, and then grandchildren as well. So God saw to it that there would always be plenty of children in the world. There's no point in creating a whole world if there are no children to keep on discovering it. That's how God goes on creating the world over and over again. He will never quite finish it, for new children keep on arriving, and they discover the world for the very first time. Yes indeed!'

The two Wise Men looked at one another.

'Well, well!' said Balthazar.

'But even though many billions of children have lived on earth, no two of them have been exactly alike,' said Impuriel. 'There are no two blades of grass in the whole of creation that are exactly alike. That's because God in heaven is so full of imagination that every now and then it bubbles over and a little spills over on to the earth.'

Joshua struck his crook against the pine tree.

'To Bethlehem! To Bethlehem!'

On they went, up through the Macedonian highlands.

The 17th of December

O N THE SEVENTEENTH OF DECEMBER Joachim woke
first. He opened the Advent calendar to find a picture
of the whole of the long procession of pilgrims on
their way down a steep mountainside.

As soon as he had unfolded the little piece of paper, Papa
and Mama came in. It was Papa's turn to read.

SERAPHIEL

It was the very end of the sixth century. Across the Macedonian
chain of mountains sped a long procession of pilgrims.

Down on the bank of the River Axios a sheep farmer raised
his eyes to the mountains and saw the seven sheep rolling
down the mountainside like a pearl necklace. Around them
fluttered a white bird. Behind the sheep came four men, one of
them holding a shepherd's crook. Behind the four shepherds
came even more people.

91

The amazing sight lasted only for a second or two, then it was gone. The Greek sheep farmer stood rubbing his eyes, but then he remembered that his father had told him once of a similar vision many years ago, when he saw a mysterious company escorted by two angels.

Long after the vision of the pilgrims' procession had gone, the sheep farmer realised that the white bird had not been a bird after all. He, too, had seen one of the angels of the Lord.

The pilgrims followed the river down to where it ran out into the Thermaic Gulf in the Aegean Sea. Elisabet had never seen such blue water.

Ephiriel pointed up at a mountain peak far away to the right of the Gulf they were gazing at.

'That's the peak of Mount Olympus. In the old days the Greeks believed the gods lived there. They were called Zeus and Apollo, Athene and Aphrodite. But now angel time tells us that 569 years have passed since the birth of Jesus, and there is no one who believes in the Greek gods any more.'

'Do they believe in Jesus?' asked Elisabet.

The angel nodded. 'But it's only a few years since the

Church closed the ancient School of Philosophy in Athens.
That was founded almost a thousand years ago by a famous
philosopher called Plato.'

'Why did they have to close the old school?'

Ephiriel said something that Elisabet hid in her heart.

'Many things have been done in the name of Jesus that
heaven is not very happy about. Jesus wanted to talk to
everyone. He never asked them to keep silent. Only a few years
later Paul came to Athens. He was the first great missionary for
Christendom, and when he arrived in Athens he wanted to talk
to the Greek philosophers. He asked them to listen to the words
of the Lord, but he wanted to hear what they thought as well.'

He couldn't say any more because Joshua struck the ground
with his shepherd's crook and said, 'To Bethlehem! To
Bethlehem!'

After a while they came to a city which stood at the
innermost point of the Gulf. Ephiriel said that the time was
551, that the city was called Thessalonica and that the Romans
had made it the capital of Macedonia.

'As early as fifty years after the birth of Jesus Paul established
a Christian community here. He was the first great missionary
for Christendom. Paul wrote two letters to the Christians in
this city. We can read them to this day, for both those letters are
in the Bible.'

Elisabet thought about the angel's words. She would not
have believed it possible to keep a few letters so long.

Then they sped further east to another city.

'This is Philippi,' said Ephiriel. 'Here Paul made his first speech on European soil, and established the first Christian community in Europe. In the Bible there is a letter he wrote to the Philippians when he was imprisoned for the sake of his faith.'

Ephiriel pointed to an octagonal church. All of a sudden one of the doors was opened from the inside. Impuriel had already started to say, 'Fear not,' when a new angel strode out of the octagonal church. He took a few steps towards Elisabet and said, 'Greetings, my daughter. I am Seraphiel, and I am coming with you to Bethlehem in order to ride on the clouds of heaven and welcome the Christ-child into the world.'

Joshua struck his shepherd's crook against the church wall. 'To Bethlehem! To Bethlehem!'

They set off along the old road between the Ionian Sea and Constantinople. Seraphiel told them that the road was called the Via Egnatia. As they ran, the angel Ephiriel said, 'The time is 511 years after Christ, and we shall be in Constantinople before it's 500.'

When Joachim came home from school, the telephone was ringing. He lifted the receiver. 'Hello?'

'It's John,' came the answer.

'Where have you been?' asked Joachim.

'I'm out in the wilderness somewhere,' replied John. 'But we can meet again another time. I just wanted to hear how things are going with the magic Advent calendar.'

'Fine,' said Joachim. 'It's almost like having a birthday every day.'

'Where has the pilgrimage got to now?' asked John.

'I think it's called Philippi,' replied Joachim. 'There are a lot of things Mama and Papa want to ask you about,' he continued. 'Can you come to coffee with us?'

John laughed. 'It's not Christmas yet.'

'You can have coffee and cakes just the same. We've baked quite a lot already.'

He was suddenly afraid that John might stop talking, so he hurried to ask, 'Are you sure the lady in the photo is called Elisabet?'

'I'm almost sure,' said John. 'If not, she's called Tebasile.'

Joachim thought of the strange Advent calendar Quirinius had given Elisabet, and of what John had said when they met by the garden gate. 'Perhaps she's called both,' he said. 'Perhaps she's called Elisabet Tebasile.'

There was a long silence.

'Yes, maybe so. Maybe so, yes!' said John at last.

'Was she Norwegian?'

'Both yes and no,' said John. 'She was from Palestine, from a little village near Bethlehem. She said she was a Palestinian refugee. But it seems she was born in Norway. The whole thing's so strange.'

'So then she ran to Bethlehem with Ephiriel and the lamb?' asked Joachim. It took his breath away.

'How you ask!' said John. 'But now I must hang up. We must learn to wait, you see Joachim. Did you know that "Advent" means something that is to come?'

And he put down the receiver.

Joachim couldn't settle to anything at home until Mama and Papa arrived. He had to tell them about the phone call over and over again, for Papa wanted to be quite sure John hadn't said anything important that Joachim had forgotten.

'Elisabet Tebasile!' he muttered. 'There can't be anyone called that.'

But there was something else. Joachim knew that a refugee was someone who had to flee from her own country because of war and danger, but he didn't know that anyone had been forced to flee from Bethlehem.

Papa told Joachim that many people in the villages around Bethlehem had had to move out of their own country because of war. Some of them had lost all their possessions and were in such difficulties that they were forced to live in refugee camps.

'A Good Samaritan should have come to help them,' said Joachim. 'Jesus wanted to teach people to help one another when any of them needed it. And then there would have been peace. For peace is the message of Christmas.'

The 18th of December

WHEN JOACHIM OPENED the magic Advent calendar on the eighteenth of December there was a picture of a rod with a shining gold ball on one end.

'That's a sceptre,' explained Mama. 'Kings and emperors have used rods like that as a symbol of dignity. The round ball is probably meant to be the sun.'

Joachim unfolded the little piece of paper that had fallen out of the calendar and read aloud to Mama and Papa. They sat on each side of him on his bed.

 THE EMPEROR AUGUSTUS

A strange procession swept through Thrace towards Constantinople on their way to Bethlehem. Five hundred years had passed since Jesus was born in a stable, swaddled in a piece of cloth, and placed in a manger because there was no room for Mary and Joseph in the inn. But that old story was already familiar in large areas of the world.

They stopped in front of one of the city gates that was guarded by soldiers. The soldiers drew their swords and raised their spears as soon as the first sheep reached the gate. Then the angel Seraphiel flew up beside the sheep and placed himself between them and the soldiers.

'Be not afraid,' he said. 'We are on our way to Bethlehem to pay homage to the Christ-child. You must allow us to pass.'

The soldiers dropped their weapons and threw themselves on the ground. One of them signalled that they could pass through the city gate. Soon all the pilgrims were inside the solid city walls.

It was early in the morning, and the city was not yet awake. The procession of pilgrims stopped on a hill with a good view of the harbour and the Bosporus which divides Europe from Asia. The sound was so narrow that they could see across to the other side.

'The time is 495,' said Ephiriel. 'Originally the city was called Byzantium, but in the year of Our Lord 330 it was made the capital of the Roman Empire by the Emperor Constantine. First he called the city New Rome, but it was soon given the name Constantinople. After that the city took back the old Greek name, Byzantium. In just under a thousand years, in 1453, the city will be conquered by the Turks, and they will give it the name Istanbul.'

'We must get across the Bosporus,' said Quirinius. 'Then it's not very far to Syria. Dixi!'

They ran down through the city and before long were standing on the furthest point of the Golden Horn. At the edge of the quay they were met by a magnificent man in colourful clothes and with a glittering sceptre in his hand. In the other hand he was holding a thick book.

'I am the Emperor Augustus and I shall accompany you across the Bosporus. I order you to accept this gesture without any unpleasant protests.'

He showed them a boat with several large sails. The sheep had already begun to jump on board.

'Then you are one of us,' said Ephiriel.

Elisabet turned to the angel and said, 'I didn't know the Emperor Augustus was a Christian.'

A mysterious smile passed over the angel's face.

'But the old Roman Emperor has been taking part in the Christmas gospel as a kind of stowaway for many centuries. And God's kingdom is open to everyone, even people who travel without a ticket.'

Elisabet thought the angel's words made heaven even bigger than she had imagined. She hid what he had said in her heart.

Soon the large company were over on the other side of the Bosporus. As they landed, Elisabet greeted the Roman Emperor and asked what kind of book he had under his arm. She thought he was going to say it was the Bible, or at any rate a hymn book, for heaven could surely demand this much of an old emperor who had suddenly decided to go along with them to Bethlehem. But the Emperor Augustus said, 'It is the sacred census.'

Joshua the shepherd thumped his crook on the ground and said, 'To Bethlehem! To Bethlehem!'

And with that they started moving down through Phrygia.

When Mama came home from work that afternoon she had a large envelope full of newspaper articles. She had been to the library to get copies of everything that had been written in the newspapers when Elisabet Hansen disappeared in 1948.

The family sat round the coffee table, reading the old newspaper cuttings. They examined the picture of Elisabet Hansen carefully. Mama took down the photo of the grown-up Elisabet from the mantelpiece and began to compare the pictures. Could the two pictures be of one and the same Elisabet?

'Both of them have fair hair,' said Mama. 'And I think they've both got a slightly pointed nose too.'

'Impossible to tell!' snorted Papa.

He was more interested in the disappearance. As he read the

old newspapers he said, 'Her mother was a teacher … her father was a well-known journalist … only her little knitted hat was found when the snow melted a few months later, in some woodland. Otherwise the police had no clues at all.'

'*They* hadn't read the magic Advent calendar,' said Joachim.

'Even if they had, they couldn't have arrested an angel,' laughed Papa. After Joachim went to bed later that evening and Mama and Papa had said goodnight, he put the light on again. It occurred to him that he hadn't looked at the large picture on the outside of the Advent calendar for several days. That was because most of the doors in the calendar had been opened. So he closed them.

THEN IT HAPPENED AGAIN!

The picture showed Mary and Joseph leaning over the baby Jesus in the manger. In the background were the Wise Men, and the angels descending through the clouds to tell the shepherds in the fields that Jesus was born.

High up on the left side there was a picture of two men in fine clothes. Unlike all the others they were standing with their backs to the scene. Joachim had seen them before, and now he was quite certain that they were supposed to be Quirinius and the Emperor Augustus. But only at this moment did he notice that the Emperor was carrying a shining sceptre.

Had he been holding a sceptre in his hand ever since Joachim was given the magic Advent calendar in the little bookshop?

Or had the sceptre drawn itself in?

O N THE NINETEENTH OF DECEMBER there was a picture of a Christmas *nisse* in the magic Advent calendar. He had long white hair and a white beard and was wearing a red cloak and a pointed red hat. On his chest hung a large silver cross set with a red stone.

Mama read what was on the little piece of paper in the Advent calendar.

MELCHIOR

A procession was speeding through Asia Minor one day towards the end of the fourth century. They travelled across the high plains of Phrygia and passed some salt lakes where the birds can stand on the water. On their long journey they encountered bears, wolves and jackals, but when a wolf or a bear came running towards them, they always managed to step aside by one or two weeks and avoid it.

They climbed up through a pass in the high mountain range of Pamphylia, which stretches from east to west along the Mediterranean coast. A couple of thousand metres above sea level they caught sight of a figure dressed in green. It was a tall man, sitting like a living landmark at the watershed where the road began tilting downwards towards the Mediterranean Sea.

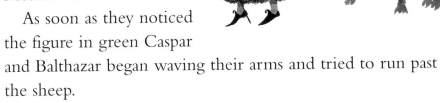

As soon as they noticed the figure in green Caspar and Balthazar began waving their arms and tried to run past the sheep.

'Who's that?' asked Elisabet.

'He must certainly be one of us,' said the angel Ephiriel.

The stranger rose and threw his arms round Caspar and Balthazar.

'The circle is complete,' he announced solemnly.

Elisabet didn't understand this, but then the stranger came over and greeted her politely as well.

'Welcome to Pamphylia,' he said. 'My name is Melchior, Third Wise Man and King of Egriskulla.'

Then Elisabet understood what he had meant by the circle being complete, for now all three Kings of Orient were gathered together.

'You have so many strange names,' she said. 'You're Wise Men, Kings of Orient, and Caspar, Balthazar and Melchior.'

Melchior smiled from ear to ear.

'We have still more names. In Greek we are called Galagat, Magalat and Sakarin. Other people call us Magi. But it doesn't matter what they call us. We are part of this story on behalf of all people on earth who do not come from the Holy Land.'

Elisabet looked up at the angel Ephiriel, and the angel nodded.

'That's quite true.'

'To Bethlehem! To Bethlehem!' said Joshua, striking a stone with his shepherd's crook.

But Melchior spoke again. 'We must greet the Christmas *nisse* first. He lives just below here.'

With which they set off down the steep mountainside towards the Mediterranean Sea. While they ran, Elisabet said, 'Is it really true that we're going to greet the Christmas *nisse*?'

Ephiriel pointed down at a town clinging to the side of the mountain. They could glimpse the Mediterranean in the background.

'The time is 322. The town is called Myra, and this is where Paul came when he was travelling to Rome to tell the capital of the Roman Empire about Jesus. He founded a Christian community in Myra too.'

'I don't understand what that has to do with the Christmas *nisse*.'

But the angel went on, 'Two hundred years after Paul came to Myra a boy was born here who was called Nicholas. His parents were Christians, and later on Nicholas was elected Bishop of Myra. In Myra there lived a girl who was very poor because her father had lost everything he owned. She wanted to get married, but it was quite impossible because she had no money for her dowry. Bishop Nicholas wanted to help the poor girl, but he knew her family were too proud to accept a gift of money.'

'Perhaps he could have put some money into her father's bank account,' suggested Elisabet.

'Yes, although this was a long time before such things as banks existed. But Nicholas did something similar. He crept out during the night and threw a bag of gold coins through their open window. In that way the girl got the money to marry after all.'

'That was kind of him.'

'But it didn't stop there. He thought it was such fun to throw gifts through people's windows that he went on doing it. When he died, many legends were told about him. Later he became St Nicholas. That turned into Santa Claus, and in Norwegian into the Christmas *nisse*. The word nisse comes from Nicholas.'

'Did he have red clothes, a long white beard and a red hat?'

'Wait and see,' said the angel Ephiriel.

The sun had not yet risen. They stopped in front of a low church building in Myra.

As soon as they stopped the church door opened. Out strode a magnificent man with a long red cloak, a long white beard, and a red hat. Round his neck he wore a large silver cross with a red stone in it. He almost looked like a Christmas *nisse*, but Ephiriel whispered in Elisabet's ear that the time was 325 years after the birth of Jesus and that the man was dressed in quite normal bishop's clothes.

'It is Bishop Nicholas of Myra,' whispered the angel.

Elisabet had an idea. 'Has it anything to do with myrrh?'

'You do well to say so, for myrrh was one of the three Christmas gifts to the Christ-child,' said the angel with a smile. 'It's become the custom to give gifts at Christmas because of the gifts the Three Wise Men brought to the Christ-child, and because of Bishop Nicholas's generosity.'

In his arms the man held three caskets. He walked firmly towards the Three Kings of Orient, bowed low, and offered each of them a casket. Caspar's casket was full of shining gold coins. In Balthazar's casket was incense, and in Melchior's casket myrrh.

'We are on our way to Bethlehem,' said Caspar.

Bishop Nicholas laughed so that his beard shook.

'Ho, ho! So you must take a few little gifts for the Child in the manger. You simply must do that, mustn't you? Ho, ho!'

Since Elisabet was standing in front of a real Christmas *nisse*, she ran right up to him and felt his red cloak. Then he bent down and lifted her up on his arm. She tried to pull his beard to find out whether it was real, and it was.

'Why are you so kind?' she asked.

'Ho, ho!' laughed the man in red again. 'The more we give away, the richer we become, and the more we keep for ourselves, the poorer we become.

That's the mystery of generosity, neither more nor less. But it's the mystery of poverty too.'

The angel Impuriel clapped his hands. 'Well spoken, Bishop!'

Bishop Nicholas continued, 'All those who lay up for themselves treasures upon earth will be poor one day, but those who have given away all they possess will never be poor. Besides, they have had great fun. Ho, ho! For the greatest joy on earth is generosity.'

'That may be so,' said Elisabet, 'but first you must own something to give away.'

At that the good-natured Bishop laughed so violently that his whole body shook.

'Not at all,' he said, when he had swallowed enough of his laughter that there was room in his mouth for speaking as well.

'You needn't own anything at all to feel generosity fizzing in your veins. A little smile is enough, or something you've made yourself.'

And with those words he put Elisabet down again on the mosaic floor in front of the church.

Joshua thumped his shepherd's crook on the ground.

'To Bethlehem! To Bethlehem!'

As they moved off they could hear the Bishop's laughter behind them in the church square.

'Ho-ho! Ho-ho! Ho-ho!'

Mama looked up from the paper and began laughing as well. It was infectious, and when Joachim burst out laughing, Papa couldn't resist it either. So they sat there chuckling, all three of them.

At last Mama said, 'I think laughter is like the wild flowers. Both are a part of the glory of heaven that has strayed down to earth. But that kind of thing is easily scattered.'

The 20th of December

O N SUNDAY THE TWENTIETH OF DECEMBER Joachim was woken by the alarm clock in Mama and Papa's bedroom. They hardly ever set the alarm for Sundays, and Joachim thought they were afraid he would wake up and open the magic Advent calendar without them. At any rate, the next moment they were both in their usual places.

'So let's get going,' said Papa.

Joachim opened the door with the number 20 on it. There was a picture of a man lying on the ground, looking up at a bright light that was shining down from heaven.

'What a curious picture,' said Mama.

But Papa was impatient. 'Let's start reading,' he said. Today it was his turn to unfold the little piece of paper and read aloud from the very tiny writing.

CHERUBIEL

A procession was on its way through Asia Minor. During the
third century it sped through Pamphylia and Cilicia south of
the high Taurus mountains, crossing rivers, orchards and
plateaux. Sometimes the pilgrims made their way along steep
slopes with old rock graves; sometimes they floundered along
the edge of the beach so that the sand spurted up around
them; sometimes they sped through Roman cities such as
Attalia, Seleucia and Tarsus. At Tarsus they paused and looked
around for a few seconds. The angel Ephiriel told them that it
was Paul's birthplace.

The mysterious procession sped round the Gulf of
Alexandretta at the very end of the Mediterranean Sea. From
now on the way to Bethlehem went south along the eastern
coast of the Mediterranean. They arrived at the Syrian city of
Antioch and stopped in front of the town gate.

'We are in the year of Our Lord 238,' said Ephiriel. 'This is where Paul's first missionary journeys began. We ought to remember, too, that the word "Christian" was used for the first time in Antioch.'

The procession of pilgrims moved off on their way to Damascus, the capital of Syria.

After a while Ephiriel called to them to stop. They were on a deserted stretch of the old Roman road through Syria.

'Here it is,' said Ephiriel, pointing at a bright red poppy at the side of the road. He continued, 'The time is 235 years after the birth of Jesus. Two hundred years ago a miracle took place here, and it was of great importance for the history of the whole world.'

The Three Wise Men lined up and bowed solemnly, and to show that he agreed, the Emperor Augustus planted his sceptre on the spot the angel had indicated.

The four shepherds tried to collect the little flock of sheep round the Emperor's sceptre. It shone like a small sun. Quirinius called their attention to the landscape and said, 'It's good to be home again. Now it's only a couple of hundred years since I was the Governor of Syria. Dixi.'

'Excuse me for asking you so directly,' said Elisabet, 'but I may be the only person who doesn't understand what you're all talking about. Jesus wasn't born here, was he?'

Ephiriel laughed.

'In the year of Our Lord 35 after Christ a Jew from Tarsus in Asia Minor was on his way to Damascus. His Roman name was Paul, but his Jewish name was Saul. As a young man he had lived in Jerusalem where he studied the ancient Jewish scriptures. He may have met Jesus there and listened to what He had to say. But Paul was a Pharisee, and the Pharisees believed that people could keep in with God by following all the laws and precepts in the Books of Moses. He became one of the enthusiastic persecutors of the Christians. He helped to throw them in prison, and even helped to kill St Stephen.'

'Then he was stupid,' said Elisabet.

Ephiriel and all the others nodded. The angel continued, 'But when he was on his way to Damascus to persecute the Christians there, he had a strange experience. Suddenly a light shone down from heaven, and Paul heard a voice saying, "Saul, Saul, why do you persecute me?" Paul asked who was calling him, and the answer was, "I am Jesus, whom you are persecuting. Get up and go into the city, and you will be told what you have to do." Paul and the men who were with him were struck speechless. All of them had heard the voice speaking, but none of them had seen anything but the light from heaven.

'Paul went in to Damascus and joined the congregation there. Before long he became the first great Christian missionary. Paul was a Roman citizen, he spoke Greek, and Aramaic which was the language Jesus spoke. And he could read the scrolls of scripture in Hebrew. On his four missionary journeys he preached about Jesus in Greece and Rome, Syria and Asia Minor.'

While Ephiriel was speaking something suddenly fell out of the sky. It happened so quickly that Elisabet didn't even have time to jump. At first she thought it was a bird that had fallen to earth because it had forgotten to beat its wings. Then she saw that a new angel was standing in front of her.

'Fear not,' said the angel. 'I am Cherubiel and I shall accompany you on the last stage of your journey to Bethlehem.'

The Emperor Augustus picked up the sceptre that had stood where Paul had heard the voice from heaven, the shepherds gave the sheep a little push, and Joshua exclaimed, 'To Bethlehem! To Bethlehem!'

Papa let the piece of paper fall on to the bed. 'Incredible!' he said.

Since it was Sunday they had plenty of time. They had already begun getting ready for Christmas: washing clothes and floors, baking cakes and colouring marzipan sweets. That day Mama and Papa did nothing but read old atlases and encyclopedias. They wanted to know about the places the pilgrims had passed through.

'I feel as if I'm back at school,' laughed Mama.

Papa read aloud from a book in the Bible called the Acts of the Apostles, where there was a lot about Paul.

It was strange for Joachim to see Papa sitting in the green rocking chair, reading the Bible. Once he put the heavy book down in his lap and said, 'This book is really quite as remarkable as the magic Advent calendar.'

As Joachim was eating his supper the phone rang. Mama took it and gave the receiver to Papa.

'Yes,' he said. 'Speaking ... Yes, quite certain. It's St Peter's in the background ... I would never have given up hope either ... All we have is this strange calendar that came to us by accident ... He's disappeared ... No I've never met him ... No, I don't believe in angels, not at all ... Of course it's possible that she was kidnapped ... It's clearly possible that she's still alive. At once, yes, I promise, and thank you for ringing.'

He put down the receiver.

'That was Mrs Hansen, Elisabet's mother,' said Papa. 'I sent her a copy of that old photo. She said the young woman could well be her daughter who disappeared, but then she was only six or seven years old. She had another daughter immediately afterwards. Her name's Anna, and she looks a little like the young woman in front of St Peter's ... '

When Papa came in to say goodnight that evening, he stood for a while with his back to Joachim, staring into the darkness outside the window.

'What on earth do you think has happened to John?'

'He's out in the wilderness,' said Joachim. 'But it's not Christmas yet.'

The 21st of December

PAPA WOKE JOACHIM early on the morning of Monday, the twenty-first of December.

Joachim sat up in bed and opened the Advent calendar.

That day there was a picture of a village beside a shining lake. The village and the low hills round the lake were bathed in gold.

Joachim unfolded the little piece of paper that had fallen out of the calendar when he opened it, and read aloud.

EVANGELIEL

Early one morning at the end of the second century after Christ the companions tumbled at top speed into. They sped past two soldiers who were guarding the western gate and sprang in along the straight street that cuts right through the city.

The soldiers turned to one another in confusion.

'What was that?'

'Only a gust of wind from the north-west.'

'But it wasn't just wind and sand. I thought I saw people as well.'

The two soldiers were reminded of an old story from a few years ago, about something that had happened at the eastern gate. A group of soldiers had been knocked over by a procession that had approached along the main street and thundered out through the city gate. It had consisted of people and animals, and one of the soldiers thought he had seen angels as well.

For as Elisabet, Ephiriel and all the others rushed out through the eastern city gate, they happened to bump into some Roman soldiers. The soldiers fell down, picked themselves up in confusion and tried to see where they had gone. But the procession was soon many years and miles away.

Late in the afternoon one day in the middle of the second century they came down to the lake of Gennesareth in Galilee. They stopped in front of a village and looked out across the shining water.

The hills lay like a wreath round the lake, and now that the golden evening sun was shining on them, Elisabet thought the lake looked like a blue china bowl, edged with gold.

The village consisted of simple houses with a small shed for livestock at one end. Between the houses walked loaded donkeys led by men wearing tunics and cloaks. The women, in loose clothing, were carrying jars on their heads.

'We are in Capernaum, which is on the old caravan trail between Damascus and Egypt,' explained Ephiriel. 'Here Jesus called His first disciples. One of them was the customs official, Matthew, for Capernaum was an important customs station. Others were the brothers Simon Peter and Andrew, who were both fishermen. "Follow me," said Jesus, "and I will make you fishers of men."'

'He helped them to catch ordinary fish too,' Impuriel hastened to add.

Joshua struck his shepherd's crook against a heap of broken stones.

'To Bethlehem! To Bethlehem!'

They sped off along the shore of the Lake of Gennesareth. Before long Ephiriel called to them to stop. He pointed up at a shelf in the rock.

'That's where Jesus gave the famous Sermon on the Mount.

He talked about the most important things He wanted to teach us.'

'So what were they?' Elisabet wanted to know.

The cherub Impuriel spread his wings, jumped up in the air and said, 'Our Father, Who art in heaven! Hallowed by Thy name. Thy Kingdom come. Thy will be done on earth as it is in heaven …

Here he was interrupted by Ephiriel.

'Yes, He taught them to pray. Above all, He wanted to teach human beings to be kind to one another. He also wanted to show that nobody is perfect in the sight of God.'

'But it's not enough to learn such rules of life by heart,' explained Melchior. 'It's more important to try to follow them. The most important thing is to do something for people in need, for people who are ill and poor, and for people fleeing from their homes. That is the message of Christmas.'

'To Bethlehem!' attempted Joshua again. 'To Bethlehem!'

They had scarcely got up speed when Ephiriel turned to Elisabet and told her that they were running through the area where Jesus had fed five thousand people with only a few loaves and fishes.

'Yes, indeed!' said Impuriel. 'Jesus wanted people to share the little they had. If only they could learn to share with each other, nobody would be hungry or poor, or very rich either. But it's better that nobody is poor and hungry than that a few people are rich.'

When they came to the village of Tiberias they turned away

from the lake of Gennesareth, up through a hilly landscape. At the head of a fertile valley with palms and fruit trees stood another village. Ephiriel called to the procession to stop.

'Angel time says 107 years have passed since Jesus was born. This town is called Nazareth. Jesus grew up here as the son of Joseph the carpenter. It was here that one of the angels of the Lord appeared to Mary and told her she was going to have a child.'

He had scarcely finished speaking when something seemed to fall down through a hole in the sky. The next moment yet another angel was standing in front of the procession. In his hand he held a trumpet. The angel blew once on the trumpet and said, 'I am the angel Evangeliel, and I proclaim to you a great joy. There is only a short time left until Jesus is born.'

Impuriel began fluttering around Elisabet.

'He is one of us and will be with us on the last part of our journey to Bethlehem.'

What had happened reminded Elisabet of the words from the old Christmas carol.

'The angel of the Lord came down
And glory shone around,'
she sang.

The Three Wise Men clapped their hands because she sang so beautifully.

That embarrassed her. So that they shouldn't all look at her, she said, 'I can see we must be getting close to Bethlehem if there are so many angels here.'

Joshua gave one of the sheep a little slap on its rump.

'To Bethlehem! To Bethlehem!'

Now there were only a hundred years to go before they reached the city of David.

Papa had sat staring in front of him while Joachim read the last lines from the piece of paper.

'Now things are starting to fall into place,' he said.

'You mean, they've arrived in the Holy Land?' said Mama.

Papa shook his head. 'Quirinius said something yesterday when they were approaching Damascus. "It's good to be home again," he said. Naturally that was because the Governor of Syria may have lived in Damascus at one time. But I seem to hear John's voice: "It's good to be home again".'

'You mean John made the magic Advent calendar, and he really does come from Damascus?' asked Mama.

Papa nodded. 'For who is Quirinius in this extraordinary story? It was Quirinius who gave Elisabet an Advent calendar, the one with the picture of the fair-haired girl. That's how he's imagined himself into the story he's telling, himself and the young woman he met in Rome. He's put it into the middle of this long story, because although Quirinius and the Advent calendar only come into the twelfth and thirteenth chapters,

Quirinius has said "Dixi" all the time when he has had something to say. That means, "I have spoken" – and I can hear John's voice again. He has spoken, and what he has said is in this remarkable Advent calendar. But an interesting bit of information came out today.'

'What's that?' asked Mama and Joachim together.

'The old flower-seller has described many towns and places on the long journey to Bethlehem, but today the description was more exact. He writes about the straight street that cuts right through Damascus from the western to the eastern gate. Only someone who's familiar with the place would write like that.'

Joachim was thinking about something quite different. He looked down at the piece of paper that he'd been reading from, put his finger on one of the sentences and said, 'The Wise Man said it's important to do something for people who are fleeing from their homes. What do you think he meant by that?'

'I suppose he was thinking of refugees and people like that,' said Papa.

'Exactly!' said Joachim. 'That's just what I thought.'

'What do you mean?' asked Mama.

'I thought it had something to do with the lady in the photo. She was a refugee too. Besides, she was his girlfriend.'

Before Joachim fell asleep that evening he sat for a while playing with the letters of the alphabet. He thought about John who had met Elisabet in Rome, and about Rome that turned into a word for love when he read it backwards.

Finally he wrote some magic letters in his notebook:

```
ELISABET
L        E
I  ROMA  B
S  O  M  A
A  M    O S
B  AMOR  I
E        L
TEBASILE
```

The diagram looked like a door – or perhaps a door that was inside another door. But what was inside *that* door?

The 22nd of December

J OACHIM WOKE UP EARLY on the morning of the twenty-second of December. There were only three days left to Christmas – and only three doors left to open in the magic Advent calendar. He was excited about what he would learn, but he didn't dare begin before his mother and father got up.

There they were, both of them. Papa seemed almost nervous. 'We'd better get going.'

Joachim opened the door and saw a picture of a man standing in a river that reached up to his waist. The upper part of his body was clothed in rags.

Mama unfolded the piece of paper and read.

THE INNKEEPER

A godly band were journeying through Samaria. It was at

the very end of the first century after Jesus' birth. They were
going to Bethlehem, to Bethlehem!

In the grey dawn one day in the year 91 they stopped at the
bank of the River Jordan, which runs from the Lake of
Gennesareth to the Dead Sea.

'Here it is!' called Ephiriel.

The angel Seraphiel took up the story.

'Out here in the wilderness Jesus was baptised by John the
Baptist. The Baptist was clad in a cloak of camel hair with a
leather belt round his waist. His food was locusts and wild honey.'

'I know that,' said Impuriel, 'for John had said, "There is one
to come who is mightier than I. I am not fit to unfasten his
sandals. I have baptised you with water, but He will baptise you
with the Holy Spirit." Then Jesus came and allowed himself to
be baptised in the River Jordan. I was sitting high up above in
the clouds, clapping my hands. It was a great moment.'

'Wasn't that when the dove came down from heaven?'
Elisabet wanted to know. She thought she had once heard
something like that.

Impuriel beat his wings and nodded. 'Yes, indeed!'

'How far is it to Bethlehem?' asked Elisabet.

'Not very far at all!' said Impuriel.

They began running again and were
soon passing a large city. As
they ran, Ephiriel
said that the city
was called Jericho

and was possibly the oldest city in the whole world.

They hurried on along the ancient road between Jericho and Jerusalem. It was the road where the Good Samaritan had helped the poor man who fell among thieves.

They stormed up to Jerusalem. First they climbed up to the Mount of Olives. They looked down at Gethsemane where Jesus had been taken prisoner by the Jews, and his disciples had slept when they ought to have been praying for Him. When they looked out over Jerusalem, Elisabet could see only ruined and destroyed buildings. Could this be the Jewish capital?

'The angel watch says it's the year 71 after Christ,' explained Ephiriel. 'Barely a year ago the Romans sacked Jerusalem and destroyed the city because its people had rebelled against the Roman colonial power. Today the Eternal City is like a shattered piece of pottery.'

'It was the Emperor Titus who did it,' said Impuriel. 'Not just him alone, of course. It was Titus and tens of thousands of soldiers.'

'They destroyed the temple as well,' continued Ephiriel. 'Only a small part of the west wall is left. Later this wall will be given the name the Wailing Wall. From this time on the Jews will be scattered over the whole world.'

They sped down through the city and ran out through the remains of the western city gate and down the road to Bethlehem. They were only a few kilometres away from the city of David.

All of a sudden they caught sight of a man who was walking

beside an ass. When he heard the procession approaching he
looked up and waved both arms.

'Fear not! Fear not!' shouted Impuriel from a long way away.

But the man was not in the least afraid.

'Then he is one of us,' said Ephiriel.

The man with the ass came towards them. He offered his
hand to Elisabet.

'I am the innkeeper. I am the
one who will say that there's
no room for Mary and
Joseph. But I shall
lend them the stable
instead.' Whereupon
he lifted Elisabet
on to the back of
the ass. 'You must be tired after your long journey,' he said.

Joshua struck his crook on the ground: 'To Bethlehem! To
Bethlehem!'

Mama put down the scrap of paper and looked at the others
with a solemn expression on her face. Papa said, 'Out here in
the wilderness Jesus was baptised by John the Baptist.'

'I know that,' said Joachim, exactly like the angel Impuriel in
the magic Advent calendar. He went on excitedly, 'John the
flower-seller is out in the wilderness too. And, he poured water
over himself and over the bookseller.'

'That can't be accidental, can it?' said Papa. 'And we never thought about his name!'

'People and flowers both need water,' Joachim went on. 'In the magic Advent calendar it said that the wild flowers are part of the glory of heaven that has strayed down to earth. I expect there was a lot of the glory of heaven in the River Jordan too.'

They had to hurry to work and to school. This was the day that Joachim's class was going to perform a nativity play for other pupils, and Joachim was going to be one of the shepherds.

On the way home the thought came to him that nearly all the pilgrims who had taken part in the long pilgrimage in the magic Advent calendar had taken part in the school nativity play as well.

As he was letting himself into the house, he noticed a letter stuck in the crack of the door. He drew it out and read the envelope. It said, 'To Joachim'!

He hurried indoors and sat down on the stool in the hall. Then he opened the letter and read:

Dear Joachim, I am inviting myself to a cup of coffee and a Christmas cookie or two on Little Christmas Eve at seven p.m. I hope the whole family will be there. Yours, John.

Joachim waited until they were sitting at the dinner table before telling Mama and Papa about the letter.

'I had a letter from John today,' he began and he ran into

his room to fetch it. He gave it to Papa, and Papa read it aloud to Mama.

'Tomorrow at seven o'clock? We must be here, then!' said Mama.

Papa grinned from ear to ear. 'For "a Christmas cookie or two"! We'll put out everything we've got. Because it's Christmas!'

The 23rd of December

'I<small>T'S</small> C<small>HRISTMAS</small>!' thought Joachim when he woke on Little Christmas Eve.

Before long Mama and Papa were awake. Papa had taken a day off work. 'Because it's Christmas,' he said again.

Joachim opened the last door but one in the Advent calendar. It was a picture of a man walking beside an ass. On the ass sat a woman in red clothes.

A piece of paper had fallen out of the calendar. Papa unfolded it and read what was written on it. Joachim could see his hand was shaking.

 MARY AND JOSEPH

A godly company was on its way to Bethlehem. In a way the procession of pilgrims stretched from the long, narrow countries below the cold North Pole at the top of Europe, right down to warm Judea, which is where Europe, Asia and Africa meet. It stretched from the distant future right back to the beginning of our era.

There were seven godly sheep, four shepherds, three Kings of Orient, five angels of the Lord, the Emperor Augustus, the Governor Quirinius, the innkeeper, and Elisabet, who was allowed to sit on the back of an ass on the last part of the journey to the city of David.

They moved along more and more slowly until they were going at an ordinary walking pace. Ephiriel said that the angel watch had stopped at the year 0. He pointed to a city far away and said that was Bethlehem.

At once the Emperor Augustus halted and put his sceptre into the ground under an olive tree. He stood up straight, opened the book he had been carrying under his arm and said in a commanding voice, 'The time has come!'

They all remained standing on the road, and the Emperor continued: 'I order you all to write your names in the census.'

He held up a piece of charcoal and handed it to each one of the pilgrims in turn. Then they all wrote their names in the big book, even the angels. Only the sheep were excused, probably because they couldn't write and nobody had given them names.

Elisabet was the last to write her name. She read out all the other names before she added her own signature.

1st shepherd: Joshua
2nd shepherd: Jacob
3rd shepherd: Isaac
4th shepherd: Daniel
1st Wise Man: Caspar
2nd Wise Man: Balthazar
3rd Wise Man: Melchior
1st angel: Ephiriel
2nd angel: Impuriel
3rd angel: Seraphiel
4th angel: Cherubiel
5th angel: Evangeliel
Quirinius, Governor of Syria
Augustus, Emperor of the Roman Empire
Innkeeper

Elisabet added her own name in this way:
1st pilgrim: Elisabet

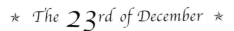

Then she had a good idea. She
thought the sheep ought to be
included in the census even though
they couldn't write and hadn't been
given any names. So she wrote:

1st sheep
2nd sheep
3rd sheep
4th sheep
5th sheep
6th sheep
7th sheep

She glanced up at the Emperor Augustus. She was afraid he might be angry because she had messed up his census, but he merely slammed the book shut.

Elisabet had worked out that there were twenty-three pilgrims listed in the census if she included herself and the seven sheep. That was as many as a whole class in school.

After they had registered, the pilgrims became a little more solemn than they had been in Copenhagen and Hamelin, in Venice and Constantinople, in Myra and Damascus.

Ephiriel said, "'Joseph went up from Galilee, out of the city of Nazareth, into Judea, unto the city of David, which is called Bethlehem (because he was of the house and lineage of David) to be taxed with Mary, his espoused wife, being great with child.'"

The procession of pilgrims started moving off slowly, but before long Ephiriel said they had to stop again. He pointed down the road. A young man was walking beside an ass, and on the ass sat a woman in red clothes. In the background Bethlehem was spread out over a terraced landscape, with long slopes almost bare of grass because of all the flocks of sheep.

'There are Mary and Joseph,' said Ephiriel. 'For now the time has come, like a ripening fruit.'

'I must hurry to get there before them,' said the innkeeper, and he started running across the hills. As he ran, he muttered to himself, 'No, I'm sorry, we're full up. But you can stay in the stable …'

A certain nervousness transmitted itself to the other pilgrims. It was as if all of them were rehearsing something they had to know by heart.

Impuriel leapt into the air, beat his wings, and said, "'Fear not: for, behold, I bring you good tidings of great joy, which shall be to all people. For unto you is born this day in the city of David, a Saviour, which is Christ the Lord. And this shall be a sign unto you; Ye shall find the babe wrapped in swaddling clothes, lying in a manger.'"

Ephiriel nodded, and Impuriel exclaimed, 'Wonderful!'

Then the angel Evangeliel blew his trumpet, and all five angels chorused together: "'Glory to God in the highest and on earth peace, goodwill toward men.'"

The sheep had suddenly begun bleating. It was as if they, too, had started practising something they had to learn by heart.

Joshua the shepherd turned to the other shepherds.

"'Let us now go, even unto Bethlehem, and see this thing which is come to pass, which the Lord hath made known unto us.'"

Finally the Wise Men spoke.

"'Where is he that is born King of the Jews? For we have seen his star in the east, and are come to worship him.'"

They knelt down and held out the caskets with gold, incense and myrrh.

The angel Ephiriel nodded with pleasure.

'I think that'll do.'

Joshua laid down his shepherd's crook carefully on the fleece of one of the sheep and whispered, 'To Bethlehem! To Bethlehem!'

Papa sat for a long time with the piece of paper in his lap before anyone dared to say anything. He had read that a certain nervousness had spread among the pilgrims as they came closer to the stable in Bethlehem. The same thing happened in Joachim's little room too.

'There can be only one Advent calendar like this in the whole world,' said Papa, 'and we're the only people to have been given it.'

Mama nodded. 'And the real Christmas night happened only once, but that Christmas night resulted in Christmas over the whole world.'

'That's because the glory of heaven spreads so easily,' said Joachim. 'I think it must be infectious.'

There was still a lot to do before Christmas Eve. The family tradition was that Mama and Papa decorated the Christmas tree on the evening of Christmas Ever, after Joachim had gone to bed, but this year they decided they would all three do it before John came. Then everything would be ready for Christmas.

Afternoon came. Mama set the table and put out all the good things they had to eat, including a big macaroon cake.

The clock was striking seven when the doorbell rang.

'You open it, Joachim,' said Mama.

He ran to the door. The old flower-seller was standing on the steps outside, smiling broadly. He held a large bouquet of roses.

'Please come in,' said Joachim.

Then Mama and Papa came and John gave Mama the roses.

'Thank you *very much*,' she said, 'and thank you for the wonderful Advent calendar.'

John put his hand on Joachim's head and replied modestly, 'I think perhaps I ought to thank *you*.'

When they were seated, John took a sip of coffee and then

began to tell them about himself.

'I was born in Damascus and grew up in a Christian home. Some people think our family goes back to the first congregation in Syria. One day when I was a boy I found an old jar containing scrolls of manuscript that were almost torn to shreds. My parents had the good sense to take it to the museum. There they discovered that the jar was very old. So were the scrolls.'

'What was written on the scrolls?' asked Papa.

'They were various reports from Roman legionaries. Amongst other things they reported something that happened in Damascus at the end of the second century after Christ. In the year 175 a curious procession is supposed to have come rushing out through the eastern city gate. A few years

later a similar procession came rushing in to the city through
the western gate. It was reported that there were some angels
in both processions.'

Mama and Joachim nodded, for they remembered what they
had read in the magic Advent calendar.

'There are many legends and myths like that from times
gone by,' continued John, 'but I was surprised that the
procession should have run *out* of the city before it ran *into* the
city. If it had, it would have had to run backwards in time, and
that's quite impossible, of course.'

'Yes, quite impossible,' agreed Papa.

'But my interest in myths and legends had been aroused. I
began to read old books, and was particularly interested in stories
about people who thought they had seen angels. Finally I had a
valuable collection of such stories, from my own part of the world
and from many countries in Europe. After some years I went to
Rome to take advantage of the treasures in the libraries there.'

'And that's where you met Elisabet?' asked Joachim.

John nodded.

'But wait a bit. I had paid attention to only a few of these
angel stories because I thought they had something in common.
They were from widely differing places, such as Hanover and
Copenhagen, Basle and Venice, the Val d'Aosta in Northern Italy
and the Axios Valley in Macedonia. But they were from very
different periods too. The earliest story was from Capernaum in
Galilee and the latest was from Norway – *that* happened on a
country road outside Halden as recently as 1916.'

'The vintage car!' said Joachim.

'Of course there are very few
people who believe such stories
these days. All the stories I had
collected said that the sight of the
little girl and the angel had lasted
only a second or two. But when
I compared the stories from
Halden, Hanover and Hamelin

with the stories from Aosta, Axios and Capernaum – well, then
those stories became quite remarkable.'

The flower-seller sat for a while, lost in his own thoughts.

'What happened to the young woman in the photo?' asked
Papa.

John sighed and Joachim thought he saw a tear in the corner
of his eye.

'Once,' he said, 'many, many years ago I met a young woman
in Rome. It was a meeting which lasted only a few weeks, but
I became very fond of her.'

'Tell us!' said Papa. 'Tell us about it!'

'She called herself Tebasile and was very secretive. She said
she was probably born in Norway, but that she had grown up
among shepherds and sheep farmers in Palestine. The latter was
certainly correct, for she spoke fluent Arabic. And the name
Tebasile sounded fairly Palestinian although it could just as
easily have been Italian.'

'But it's Elisabet backwards!' exclaimed Joachim.

John nodded. 'Yes, you're a sharp one, you are. People don't usually spell their names backwards.'

'Go on!' begged Papa.

'It might have been true that she was Norwegian as well. Her skin was fair, almost peach-coloured, and her eyes were blue and sparkling. When I asked what took her to Palestine she just sat staring into my eyes. She said, "I was kidnapped." I had to ask who had kidnapped her, and she replied, "An angel who needed me in Bethlehem … but it's so long ago … I was only a little girl …".'

Mama gasped.

'What did you say?' asked Papa.

'Other people would probably merely have smiled at such a pack of lies. But I thought of all my angel stories. I replied that I believed what she told me. But the very fact that I took her seriously must have scared her.'

'What happened next?' asked Mama.

'We saw each other only once after that. It was on the Way of Reconciliation in front of St Peter's Square. She said she would be leaving Rome the same afternoon. But she let me take a picture of her. That was in April 1961.'

'How did *you* come to Norway?' asked Papa. 'And why?'

John took the top ring of the macaroon cake and said, 'I came here because I hoped to meet that mysterious woman again, and since then I've stayed here. But I've never met her. I've never managed to find the answer to where she might be. But we'll see …'

He took a bite of the little macaroon ring.

'It wasn't long before I heard about that disappearance in 1948. That was when I began asking myself whether the poor little girl could have been Tebasile, who had said she was kidnapped by an angel when she was a small child. I didn't know exactly how old she was, but it could fit if she had been born in about 1940.'

John was silent for a while. Then he said, 'I noticed the strange similarity in the names only recently. During the early years in Norway I thought about Tebasile almost continually. Then it struck me like a bolt from the blue. When I read her name backwards, it turned into Elisabet! I became even more convinced that I really had met the missing Elisabet all those years later in Rome. That was when I began to make the magic Advent calendar. I was many months making it, you understand.'

'Then you put a picture of Elisabet in the shop window,' said Mama.

John nodded. 'To see whether anyone here in town would recognise her.'

'Why did you travel to the wilderness?' Joachim wanted to know.

And the old flower-seller explained.

'Every Advent I go out to the country and walk in the woods and hills outside town. To find peace before the Christmas festival, but also to see whether I can find any trace of the lamb, Elisabet and the angel Ephiriel who set off for Bethlehem in 1948. I admit it. Sometimes I walk about saying the two names inside my head: Elisabet … Tebasile … Elisabet.'

'Have you never wanted to go back to Damascus?' asked Papa.

John shook his head.

'No, this is my home now. I sell flowers at the market, and in that way I can help to spread a little of the glory of heaven around me. That sort of thing is very easily scattered, you know. And one day Elisabet may come back to town. Because there's something else …'

It was so quiet in the room that they could almost hear dust flakes falling on to the wooden floor.

John said to Joachim, 'All these years I've tried hard to find her again. But I knew only her first name, or so I believed. To find an Elisabet or a Tebasile only by her Christian name – whether in Rome or in Palestine – well, that's more difficult than to catch a sparrow in your hand. I've been laughed at in embassies and in census offices in quite a few countries. But Joachim …'

Again it was completely silent in the room.

'Joachim may have helped me to find her again. So I'm the one to thank *you*.'

Joachim looked up at Mama and Papa. He couldn't fathom what John was talking about.

'I think you'll have to explain a bit more,' said Mama.

'It was Joachim who set me to thinking that maybe she had both names, one as her first name and the other as her last name.'

Joachim's face lit up. 'Elisabet Tebasile!' he said. 'Is *that* what she's called?'

'There's a telephone subscriber in Rome who has that name. But it's not Christmas yet. Tomorrow you must open the last door in the magic Advent calendar.'

John got to his feet and said he had to hurry because there was something he had to do.

'But maybe I can have a look at the Advent calendar for the last time?' he said.

Joachim rushed into his bedroom and took the magic Advent calendar down from its hook. When he was back in the sitting room he handed the calendar to John, who stood examining the picture.

'You must push all the open doors shut,' explained Joachim.

So that's what he did. He said, 'Yes, here they all are. Quirinius and the Emperor Augustus, the angels in the sky and the shepherds in the fields, the Kings of Orient and Mary, Joseph and the Christ-child.'

'But not Elisabet,' said Joachim.

'No, not Elisabet.'

They accompanied John to the door. As he was about to leave, he said, 'So we'll have to see what this Christmas will bring.'

'Indeed, we shall,' said Papa. He was clearly relieved to have finally heard the flower-seller's story.

But John said something more.

'You won't open the last door in the Advent calendar until the bells ring Christmas in tomorrow afternoon, will you?'

Mama looked at him. 'No-o-o, I suppose not.'

'No, we'll have to try to wait that long,' decided Papa.

When John was on the steps outside, he said, 'Maybe I'll knock on your door tomorrow as well.'

Joachim was delighted. He felt something bubbling and fizzing deep down inside him. That was because John had said that maybe he'd look in tomorrow too. For Joachim was not as pleased about everything as Mama and Papa were.

Something was still missing, it seemed to him.

The 24th of December

CHRISTMAS EVE BEGAN AS USUAL. There was always some last-minute task that had to be done, and last-minute presents to be wrapped up. Now and again Mama or Papa would sneak into Joachim's room and glance expectantly at the magic Advent calendar. They had promised not to open it until the bells rang Christmas in.

Later in the day they began to prepare Christmas dinner. Before long the whole house was smelling of Christmas. At last it was five o'clock. Papa opened a window, and now they could hear the church bells ringing.

Nobody said anything, but they all crept into the bedroom. Joachim climbed on to the bed and opened the last, big door in the calendar. It was the one that covered the manger with the

Christ-child. The picture beneath it showed a cave in a mountain.

For the last time they sat on the edge of the bed. Joachim unfolded the thin sheet of paper and read aloud to Mama and Papa.

 ## THE CHRIST-CHILD

It's the middle of the world between Europe, Asia and Africa. It's the middle of history at the beginning of our era. Soon it will be the middle of the night as well.

A silent crowd is stealing upwards between the houses in Bethlehem. They are a little flock of seven sheep, four shepherds, five angels of the Lord, three Kings of Orient, one Roman Emperor, the Governor of Syria, and Elisabet from the long, narrow country below the North Pole.

The weak glow of oil lamps is streaming from the windows in a few of the simple houses, but most people in the old town have gone to bed for the night.

One of the Wise Men points up at the sky where the stars are burning in the darkness. They are like sparks from a beacon far away. One star is shining more brightly than all the other stars in the sky. It looks as if it's hanging a little lower in the sky as well.

'O little town of Bethlehem,
How still we see thee lie.
Above thy deep and dreamless sleep
The silent stars go by,'

murmurs Elisabet softly, remembering an old carol.

The angel Impuriel turns towards the others, puts a finger to his lips, and whispers, whispers, 'Hush … Hush …'

The procession of pilgrims gathers in front of one of the inns of the town. In a moment or two the innkeeper appears at the window. When he sees the group outside he nods firmly and points to a cave in the wall of rock.

The angel Ephiriel whispers something; it sounds like the words of a nursery rhyme.

'"And while they were there, the time came for her child to be born, and she gave birth to her son, her first-born. She wrapped him in swaddling clothes, and laid him in a manger, because there was no room for them in the inn."'

They creep across the yard and stop in front of the cave. The smell from it tells them that it is a stable.

Suddenly the silence is broken by the cry of a child.

It is happening now. It is happening in a stable in Bethlehem.

Over the stable a star is twinkling. Inside the stable the new-born child is wrapped in swaddling clothes and laid in a manger.

This is a meeting of heaven and earth. For the child in the manger is also a spark from the great beacon behind those weak lanterns in the sky.

This is the wonder. It is a wonder every time a new child comes into the world. This is how it is when the world is created anew under heaven.

A woman is breathing deeply and weeping. Not out of sadness. Mary is weeping quietly, deeply and happily.

But the child's cries drown out Mary. The Christ-child is born. He has been born in a stable in Bethlehem. He has come to our miserable world.

The angel Ephiriel turns solemnly towards the other pilgrims and says, "'Unto you is born this day in the city of David a Saviour.'"

The Emperor Augustus nods.

'And now it's our turn. Everyone is to take up their places, everyone must remember their lines. We have rehearsed this for almost two thousand years.'

Quirinius speaks, at a sign from the Emperor.

'Shepherds! Take your flock out into the fields, and never forget to be Good Shepherds. Wise Men! Depart to the desert and mount your camels, each one of you. May you never cease to read the stars in the sky. Angels! Fly high above the clouds, all of you. Do not reveal yourselves to people on earth unless it is absolutely necessary, and never forget to say, "Fear not!" For now Jesus is born.'

The next moment all the shepherds and sheep, the angels and the Wise Men, had vanished. Elisabet was left alone with Quirinius and the Emperor Augustus.

'I must hurry home to Damascus,' said Quirinius. 'I have an important role to play there.'

'And I must go back to Rome,' said Augustus. 'That is my role.'

Before they went, Elisabet pointed at the stable and asked, 'Do you think I may go in?'

The Emperor smiled from ear to ear.

'Of course you are to go in. That is your role.'

Quirinius nodded energetically.

'You haven't come all this long way just to hang about.'

With those words the two Romans started running back along the way they had come.

Elisabet looked up at the starry sky. She had to tilt her head far back to see the big star which was shining so brightly. Again she heard the cry of a child from inside the cave.

So she went into the stable.

Papa got up from the bed and punched Joachim on the shoulder. 'Well, we certainly took a remarkable Advent calendar home with us this year,' he said.

He seemed to have finished with it all.

Joachim wasn't as pleased as he was. For what had happened to Elisabet? Mama sat for a while, thinking too. When she got to her feet at last, she said, 'Christmas dinner will be ready soon. Perhaps you could put the presents under the tree while we're waiting. There are a few little surprises this year as well.'

That was exactly what she said. Then the doorbell rang. It was Joachim who opened it again, and again old John was standing outside. Today he was beaming even more than yesterday.

'I've come just to thank you,' he said.

Mama and Papa hurried up and beckoned him in. The macaroon cake was put out on the table again. Only the topmost ring was missing. Papa had put a ball of red marzipan on it instead. Joachim brought out coffee cups and plates.

They sat round the coffee table and John looked at all three of them in turn. He had a mysterious expression on his face.

'When I drew the large picture on the magic Advent calendar,' he said, 'I tried to do it in such a way that there would always be something new to discover. All God's creation was like that, I thought. The more we understand, the more we see in things around us, and the more we see in things around us, the more we understand. So there will always be something new to discover if we only have our eyes and ears open to the remarkable world we live in.'

Papa nodded, and John went on, 'But I didn't know that the calendar was made so that the person who read the scraps of paper would also solve the old mystery of the little girl who disappeared from town almost fifty years ago.'

'Have you found out something more about Elisabet?' asked Joachim. But John didn't have time to answer, for the next moment the doorbell went again.

Mama looked at Papa, and Papa looked at Mama.

'You'd better open it, Joachim,' said John. 'I expect you're the person who has opened all the doors in the magic Advent calendar. Now you must open this last door as well. But you must open it from the inside.'

When he opened the front door a woman aged about fifty was standing there. She was wearing a red coat and had fair hair with a little grey in it. The woman gave him a big smile and held out her hand.

'Joachim?' she said.

Joachim felt a bit dizzy but he knew who she was, so he shook her hand.

'Elisabet Hansen,' he said. 'Won't you come in?'

When they came into the sitting room the old flower-seller gave up keeping a straight face and burst out laughing. Joachim thought he was a bit like Bishop Nicholas in the magic Advent calendar.

Elisabet was left standing in the middle of the room with her red coat over her arm. Round her neck she was wearing a silver cross set with a red stone.

When John at last managed to stop laughing, he got up from his chair and said, 'Perhaps I should introduce you. This is Elisabet Tebasile Hansen – one and the same person. I came a few minutes ahead of her, but here she is.'

Mama and Papa looked confused, so just in case, Joachim stood in front of them and started to flap his arms. 'Fear not!' he said. 'Fear not! Fear not!'

Only then did they get up from the sofa to shake Elisabet's hand. Mama took her coat and brought another chair, Papa went to fetch another coffee cup from the kitchen.

It appeared that she spoke only English. When they had all sat down again, Papa spoke in Norwegian all the same.

'I think I must ask for an explanation,' he said. 'I think I must almost demand a proper explanation.'

'And I'll give it in Norwegian, for the boy's sake,' said John. 'It's to his credit that we are all able to be here today.'

It looked as if the woman with the necklace understood what he was saying, for she looked down at Joachim and smiled.

'Go on!' said Papa.

'When I came to see you yesterday I knew already that Elisabet was on her way to Norway,' began the flower-seller.

'Why didn't you tell us?' cried Mama.

John chuckled. 'One doesn't open a Christmas present before Christmas Eve. Besides, I couldn't be quite sure whether she really would come. I couldn't even be quite sure who would be coming.'

John explained what had happened.

'It began several days ago when I talked to Joachim on the phone. For many years I've tried to trace either a certain Elisabet or a certain Tebasile – for I was convinced that she was one and the same person. But it was Joachim who hinted to me that perhaps Elisabet used Tebasile as her last name. I called Information, was given a telephone number in Rome, and rang her. It didn't take long for her to remember me from those magic days in April 1961.'

Elisabet tried to say something, but John interrupted her with a wave of his hand.

'I told her the story of a mother who had

lost her child in 1948. That's how I could tell her who she was. She came to town late yesterday evening. She has not set foot in this place since she disappeared that December day forty-five years ago.'

Papa jumped up from the sofa and went to the phone.

'What is it?' asked Mama.

'I promised to phone Mrs Hansen as soon as I heard anything new.'

John laughed. 'Elisabet stayed with her mother last night. They scarcely closed their eyes, but everything is in good order, I assure you.'

'May I ask a question?' Papa said. 'Exactly what did happen in December 1948? And don't tell me that Elisabet set off after a lamb and met an angel called Ephiriel.'

He turned towards Elisabet and asked her the same question in English. She put a hand to her mouth to keep back an explosion of laughter, and signed to John that he should answer.

'She always begins to laugh when we talk about that,' explained John. 'We can't agree on it. I'll give you Elisabet's explanation first. She thinks the police in this town did a very bad job. But I think we should begin at the other end.'

'Begin at whatever end you like, as long as you can get the ends to meet,' said Papa.

'Elisabet grew up in a little village near Bethlehem,' said John. 'The people there lived off the poor land they tilled, but even this poor land was taken away from them. When I met Elisabet in Rome in the spring of 1961 she had lived in different refugee camps, first in Jordan, afterwards in Lebanon. She went to Rome in order to explain the refugees' situation. Well, never mind, we can talk about that later. But Elisabet really did go to Bethlehem in December 1948. She came to poor, persecuted people who needed God's help. That's what she meant when she said she had been kidnapped by an angel. She meant she had been kidnapped by someone who wanted to help the people in the villages round Bethlehem. She grew up there as a shepherd girl, so she was able to stroke the soft fleece of the lambs at an early age – just like Elisabet Hansen in the magic Advent calendar.'

'So she suddenly disappeared in Rome,' said Papa. 'Why didn't she want to see you again?'

'I've asked myself that question many times in the years that have passed since then. The answer is that she had to be very careful about who she talked to. That was why she turned her name upside down and took Tebasile as her surname. We mustn't forget that there was a war in the country she came from. Elisabet was afraid of being kidnapped again.'

'Go on!' said Papa.

'When I told her I believed her angel story her suspicions were aroused. She was afraid I might be a dangerous person where her own safety was concerned, and for the Palestinian people.'

'But wasn't Elisabet Norwegian?' Mama wanted to know.

'Yes, she was Norwegian,' answered John. 'Elisabet thinks she was kidnapped by some very unhappy people who were willing to do almost anything so that the world should have its eyes opened to the suffering of the Palestinian people.'

'All the same, it was dreadful to kidnap an innocent child,' said Mama.

'Of course you're quite right. Elisabet thinks they must have intended to take her back. Perhaps the people who kidnapped her wanted to try to get her father to write in the papers about all the people who were driven from village to village and finally herded into huge refugee camps outside their own country.'

'So why wasn't she taken back?' interrupted Papa.

'Elisabet says she remembers very little until she was looked after by a big family in the tiny village outside Bethlehem.'

'And what is your explanation?' asked Mama.

'You know what that is already,' said John.

Joachim was sitting on the edge of his chair.

'You think she did follow the lamb with the bell and met the angel Ephiriel in the woods?' he asked.

John nodded. 'I still do.'

'No!' said Elisabet.

'Yes!' said John.

'No!' said Elisabet, and laughed.

The others began laughing too.

'You mustn't start quarrelling,' said Joachim.

'I believe Elisabet's story,' said Papa.

'And what about you?' asked John, looking at Mama and Joachim.

'I believe twenty-four times more in John's story,' said Joachim.

'Then I'll have to vote twelve times for John's story and twelve for Elisabet's,' decided Mama. 'Because I think a few angels have flown to Bethlehem this Christmas. And back again here, for that matter.'

'But Joachim is right when he says we mustn't start quarrelling even though we believe slightly different things,' said John. 'That's the message of Christmas too. Maybe it's the greatest of all truths that the glory of heaven is easily scattered – at least, if we humans share in dividing it out. When I wrote on those scraps of paper that I folded up so carefully and put inside the magic Advent calendar I had a few clues. I had heard about Elisabet Hansen who disappeared, and I had met Tebasile in Rome. And I had the old angel stories to rely on as well. The rest of it I had to imagine myself.'

Silence fell in the sitting room.

'You managed it very well,' said Mama.

John smiled shyly. 'The imagination, also, is a tiny piece of the glory of heaven that has strayed down to earth. It, too, can be scattered very easily.'

'It's all amazing,' said Mama. 'We open the last door in an old Advent calendar and hear about Elisabet who goes into a stable in Bethlehem to welcome the Christ-child into the world. Immediately afterwards the same Elisabet rings the doorbell in

our own house. So it almost seems as if this house is the same
as the stable where Jesus was born.'

She stood up and put her arms round Elisabet. 'Welcome
back to Norway, my child,' she said.

That was a funny thing to say, since Elisabet was almost
twenty years older than Mama.

'Thank you very much,' said Elisabet, and she said those
words in Norwegian.

Before long Elisabet and John had to leave. But they would
all meet again after Christmas because Mama and Papa and
Joachim had been invited to a big Christmas party at home
with Elisabet's family.

The guests were escorted to the front door. Outside it was
snowing heavily.

Papa asked whether Elisabet could remember any Norwegian
from when she was small.

She stood under the outside light
while the snow poured down on to her
red coat. Suddenly she bent down and
stretched out her hand as if she was
trying to catch the dancing snowflakes.

'Lambkin, lambkin, lambkin!' she said.
She put her hand up to her mouth
in alarm. The next moment she
started running. A few seconds
later she and the old flower-
seller were gone.

Late that evening, when Joachim was going to bed, he stood for a long time in front of his window, staring out into the Christmas night. There had been a huge fall of new snow, but now it was clear enough to see the stars.

Suddenly he caught sight of some figures running past down on the road. It was not easy to keep his eyes on them, for he could see them only in the light of the street lamps, and the sight lasted for only a second or two.

Joachim thought he had recognised the angel Ephiriel and all the others who had accompanied Elisabet to Bethlehem.

That night they had escorted her back.